"This first novel by Isabelle weaves together the world of resilient spiritof Angelique the protagonist. With its richly imagined settings and beautifully written prose, this story not only celebrates diversity but also showcases transformative power."
Prof. Phan Nhuan David

"Angelique's rapid rise from ordinary woman to Queen of the Underworld had me gripped from the first page. Sakola is a unique and compelling read."
Ed Power

"The story is well written, with great descriptions but not too many. The dialogues are good and funny at times."
Elvira Sepulveda-Duran

SAKOLA

QUEEN OF THE UNDERWORLD

Copyright © 2023 Isabelle Kamalandwa Bryan

The moral right of the author has been asserted.

Apart from any fair dealing for the purposes of research or private study, or criticism or review, as permitted under Copyright, Design and Patents Act 1998, this publication may only be reproduced, stored or transmitted, in any form or by any means, with prior permission in writing of the publishers, or in any case of the reprographic reproduction in accordance with the terms of licences issued by the Copyright Licensing Agency. Enquiries concerning reproduction outside these terms should be sent to the publishers.

PublishU Ltd

www.PublishU.com

All rights of this publication are reserved.

Thanks

I am grateful for all who have encouraged and supported me in this journey. I am also thankful to PublishU for guiding me through the process of writing and helping me to birth this story of Sakola that had been simmering in my loins for a number of years.

Finally, to every reader of this book, thank you for giving me permission to take you on this incredible adventure.

Contents

Chapter 1	Goodbye Laurent
Chapter 2	Angelique's dream
Chapter 3	Richard's funeral
Chapter 4	Queen Sorceress Funke – The Prophecy
Chapter 5	Angelique meets Ma'Dika
Chapter 6	The initiation
Chapter 7	A trip to Metropolis
Chapter 8	Amazonia and Mammon
Chapter 9	Family feud
Chapter 10	Angelique marries Abaddon
Chapter 11	Hello Laurent
Chapter 12	The proposal
Chapter 13	Meet the Janssens
Chapter 14	Greta's past
Chapter 15	What Greta did not know
Chapter 16	The execution
Chapter 17	Abaddon's big plan
Chapter 18	The Matchmaking Game
Chapter 19	Greta's obsession

Chapter 20	Rachel's Dream
Chapter 21	Rachel won't budge
Chapter 21	Plan B
Chapter 23	Hello Santi baby
Chapter 24	Ludovic and Erika
Chapter 25	Woman scorned
Chapter 26	The dowry
Chapter 27	Tragedy for love
Chapter 28	No weapon formed
Chapter 29	Old Allies
Chapter 30	Intel is key
Chapter 31	Abaddon's threat
Chapter 32	Angelique strikes
Chapter 33	The punishment
Chapter 34	Who is the Bright Morning Star?
Chapter 35	Goodbye love
Chapter 36	Brownie's Triumph

SAKOLA

ISABELLE KAMALANDWA BRYAN

Chapter 1
Goodbye Laurent

"You haven't forgotten anything?" asked Laurent as he was zipping the medium size Louis Vuitton suitcase.

"No," uttered Angelique under her breath, gazing past the back garden through the window of the living room.

She looked tiny and vulnerable in her white vest, pair of blue jeans, knee-length UGG boots and braids falling from her shoulders down to her waist. The spring sun caressed her beautiful brown skin as she stood leaning on the windowsill with her arms folded.

Laurent turned to her and said "Come here". He opened his arms and held them out to her. She slowly walked to him, hid her face in his chest and sobbed bitterly. Laurent held on tight as her body quivered in his arms.

The sound of a horn blowing outside signalled the arrival of the taxi they had been waiting for. They pulled apart, Angelique wiped away her tears with the back of her hand, whilst Laurent took her suitcase and carried it outside where the cab driver was waiting.

While Laurent loaded her luggage in the boot of the taxi, Angelique grabbed her black tailored jacket on her way out, checked that her passport was in her bag and came out of her student terrace house in Bedford, East of England.

"You know if I did not have this thesis to submit, I would have come with you?" said Laurent to Angelique as he held her face with both hands.

"I know," she replied.

She looked up at him with her big dove brown eyes, filled with sadness. He leaned down and kissed her gently. His lips locked onto hers for one long minute. Right then, he shared his girlfriend's pain with a kiss.

"Je t'aime," he whispered.

"Moi aussi je t'aime," she answered back softly.

Angelique Sakola was very fond of Laurent Chevalier. He was just her type, tall, green eyes, wavy fair hair and a smile that would make any girl go weak at the knee. On top of that, he was able to challenge her intellectually. She loved their debates on politics and the global economy. She got a sense of pride walking around campus on his arm under the envious glare of most girls who would have gladly stepped in her shoes. Well, she might as well admit it, although what she had with Laurent looked a lot like love, he was also undeniably the best catch on campus. One word: trophy-boyfriend!

They met at Cranfield University while studying for their Master's degrees; Angelique in Business Administration and Laurent in Environmental Econometrics. They made an exotic couple, a six foot two inch white male with a five foot three inch petite black female. For sure, they attracted attention wherever they went.

Interestingly, however, it was not love at first sight for Angelique. Laurent, on the other hand, felt an instant attraction from the first time he laid eyes on her three years ago. He was drawn to her larger-than-life personality, delicate facial features and curvaceous physique epitomised by a worthy-of-an-award derrière.

Nonetheless, he patiently bided his time before making his move. They started as good friends and the friendship grew into a full-blown relationship some months later. So, there they were.

Angelique got into the black cab, shut the door as Laurent stood by the roadside. She waved at him; he blew her a kiss, both unaware that life as they knew it would never be the same again. Fate had other plans.

ISABELLE KAMALANDWA BRYAN

Chapter 2
Angelique's Dream

"Dad, what's this place? I don't like it." Angelique looked around her. They were surrounded by nothing but scattered trees and grassy woodland for as far as Angelique's eyes could see. It was night-time. The darkness was deep, eased only by the glow of the full moon and yellow eyes of owls piercing through the twilight. The scene resembled that of a horror movie. It felt rather surreal and creepy. Angelique was petrified.

She stood facing her father by the largest tree she had ever seen. It was over 100 feet tall and leafless. It had a barrel-like broad trunk that gave rise to thick tapering branches resembling an intricate root system, which grabbed part of the moon. It was the legendary African baobab tree.

Angelique had no recollection of how they both got to that place. She just found herself there.

"Don't be afraid, sweetheart; everything will be fine." Richard put a hand on Angelique's cheek in a bid to reassure her. After all, he needed her to be calm to proceed with the handover of the Sakola Totem.

He continued reassuring her, "I am with you, so nothing bad will happen to you. Do you trust me?"

"Yes, dad, I do," she responded. Her dad was her hero. There was no one she admired more than him. She would follow him till the end of the earth if need be. So, she managed to calm herself down, and the environment did not feel as spooky anymore. Seeing that his daughter had regained composure, Richard broke out disturbing news to her, saying, "I'll be going away soon".

"What do you mean, where?" Angelique was intrigued.

"Nowhere too far, but when the time comes, I need you to do everything Ma'Dika asks you to do." There was a sense of urgency in the tone of his voice.

"Who is Ma'Dika?" Angelique was getting increasingly confused.

Richard stroked his daughter's hair with a warm smile and said, "It will all make sense very soon; just promise me you'll do what you're told."

Angelique hesitated at first, then softly declared, "I promise."

Richard took a cola nut out of his pocket, broke it and gave some to his daughter, "now eat this!" he ordered.

Angelique took the piece of cola nut and ate it. It was bitter and dry, she hated the taste of it, but she bravely chewed it and managed to swallow it.

When she was done, Richard smiled with satisfaction, "That's my girl."

He held out a fifteen inch ivory tusk carved with depictions of a crocodile, a bull, a leopard and an owl processing in a spiral, with the tip terminating with a carved jackal's head. Attached at the bottom end was a black and white tail of a Zebra.

"Take this!" he commanded. "This is our totem, the emblem of our clan. It's now in your care like it was in mine and our ancestors who preceded us."

Angelique took the tusk with a shaking hand. Richard bowed on one knee and praised her, "Hail Chief Sakola."

Angelique was unsure about what to make of this ritualistic act. Richard got back on his feet, placed a hand on his daughter's head, lifted his eyes and declared ceremoniously with a strong voice, "Oh master of the bottomless pit, Great King Abaddon. I have fulfilled my vow. She is yours. Now oh great king, bring to pass the prophecy of dominion for the Sakola name that was spoken by your soothsayers".

If she was confused before, Angelique was totally lost now; she had no clue what was happening.

Richard hugged his daughter and smiled again. Angelique reciprocated the hug, albeit nervously. She was glad that he seemed pleased with her. However, upon looking closely at Richard, Angelique detected, in spite of the pitch blackness of the night, unexplainable fear in her father's eyes. Suddenly two black-green eight feet tall ghostly heavy built creatures with lizard skin surged out of the baobab, apprehended Richard and dragged him inside the tree. Angelique reached out to her dad as the grunting beings carried him away, but they were as fast as a flash, and in a blink of an eye, they had disappeared before her eyes into the baobab. She hit the tree with her fists whilst tears of desperation streamed down her face, shouting, "Dad! Dad! Give me back my dad, somebody, please help me, Daaaaaaaaaad!"

"Miss Sakola, Miss Sakola," the air hostess was gently shaking Angelique's right shoulder, "please wake up, wake up..."

Angelique opened her eyes, gasping for air. Her heart was pounding. It was that dream again.

"Thank you," she said softly.

"You're welcome. You were shouting; it must have been a bad dream. Shall I bring you something to drink, a glass of water perhaps?"

Angelique shook her head, "No, thank you." She was not thirsty.

The stewardess smiled and carried on attending other customers in the first-class section of the flight to Kinshasa, the capital of Congo.

It was that same dream she had the night before she got the ill-fated phone call informing her of the sudden death of her father.

Angelique fixed her eyes on the plane's window as the expert pilot manoeuvred its landing on the capital's international airport runway. The humid tropical heat engulfed her entire being as she set foot on her motherland. Her two sisters were waiting at the arrival gate, dressed in black, their countenance heavy with grief. The moment Angelique appeared, they walked over to her and clung to her, crying and wailing for their father. Angelique wept silently. As the first born, it was her duty to be strong.

Chapter 3
Richard's Funeral

"That was a lovely ceremony, I am so glad everything went well and your father was buried in peace with honour," said Oluchi, Angelique's mother, who breathed a sigh of relief sitting at the back of the limousine in the company of Angelique and younger non-identical twin sisters; Lena and Linda. Oluchi did not take it lightly that no trouble had erupted; in fact, she was grateful. Often, whenever a wealthy man of Richard's status died in their tribe, the in-laws would usually attempt to gain ownership of the defunct wealth and leave the widow and children destitute. Therefore, the very fact that no one from Richard's family had incited such a stir was something for Oluchi and her children to be thankful for.

Angelique paid little attention to her mum's remarks, too preoccupied striving to reconcile within herself that her father was no more and she would never see him again. Her hero was gone. Richard was her voice of wisdom. They had similar personalities and interests. He left an unusual void in her life that no one could fill.

The twins, on the other hand, were keen to share their own observations. "You're right, mum. It was serene," Lena agreed with her mother. "But did you see Sam? He makes me so uncomfortable that guy; he looked so evil."

Sam was the Sakola's girls' half-brother. Oluchi endured years of unexplained barrenness following her marriage to Richard. Thus, faced with continuous pressure from his family for a male heir, Richard married a second wife,

Marie Mbanda, with whom he fathered two children; Sam and Sandra. Feeling defeated by her rival's success in bearing two children, Oluchi had made peace with herself that she would be childless, until one day as if by miracle Angelique was conceived and then the twins.

Strangely, despite having a male child, the family was perplexed when Richard decided that Angelique would receive the first-born rights instead of Sam. He ensured that his testament clearly stipulated his wishes. Richard was an extremely wealthy man. His allegiance to the one-party and authoritarian regime of Congo enabled him to amass a colossal personal fortune through a system of corruption and the exploitation of the country's natural resources for personal gain. Therefore, Angelique was named chairwoman and seventy-five per cent majority shareholder in Richard's petroleum company, whilst the twins were handed the remaining twenty-five per cent divided equally among them. Richard deliberately excluded Sam and Sandra from inheriting his multi-million dollars energy company, foreseeing the friction that would be engendered should the half siblings be forced to work together. However, they were not left penniless. Some years preceding his death, Richard had acquired a small construction firm which he grew into a respectable medium-size business owning approximately a forty per cent share of the Congolese construction market. He felt it more appropriate to leave that company to Sam and Sandra, with Sam as the seventy-five per cent majority shareholder. Richard also bequeathed property to each one of his children located in the most prestigious neighbourhoods in Kinshasa. In relation to his wives, the main family home went to Oluchi, and Marie, the secondary house, which Richard purchased when they married.

Inside the limousine, Linda picked up on her sister's comment, "I agree with you, Lena, it just feels like he doesn't like us and at the funeral, he looked like he hated us even more."

"Don't you worry about it; I am sure it's just your imagination," Oluchi was attempting to diffuse any tension from brewing between hers and Marie's household.

However, Oluchi had failed to realise or maybe just chose to turn a blind eye to the reality that both sides were past just mere tension, and the situation was sliding into war mode. Indeed, Sam was seething with rage. He could not care less about the construction company because what the non-enlightened members of the family were oblivious to was that the most coveted part of the inheritance had slipped from his hands, and that was the Sakola Totem.

Richard Sakola came from a long lineage of chiefs from the Mutambus tribe. Tribal chiefs carried great political and spiritual authority in the country and were gifted with dark powers and occult knowledge from the ancestors of the land, which is passed from one generation to another.

Marie's union with Richard was sealed by Ma'Dika, the most renowned witch doctor in the whole of the southern region of Congo. Being from the same tribe as Richard, unlike Nigerian Oluchi, Marie was told that should she bear a male child; he'd succeed Richard as the chief of the tribe. She often relayed that promise to Sam, who harboured the expectation of being called one day Chief Sakola.

In their tradition, a chief would hand over the totem to their chosen heir, a blood child, shortly before breathing their last. Sam did not get summoned by Richard prior to his passing and now that he was six feet under, it was crystal clear that the Chief seat had gone to another one of Richard's children. Although he had no proof yet, he suspected that the chosen child was Angelique. He felt cheated out of what he knew to be rightfully his. But the question both on his and Marie's mind was what drove Richard to select a female as the next chief of tribe, especially since it was against the custom of the Mutambus. A female chief was considered an abomination. Notwithstanding, he was determined to recover the totem prior to the coronation which traditionally took place seven days after the deceased chief's burial.

Chapter 4
Queen Sorceress Funke – The Prophecy

The crow of the rooster woke up Ma'Dika. She sat on her mat, it still looked quite dark. The sun had not quite risen yet. That rooster started early today, she thought. She needed a wee anyway so she made her way towards the external latrine.

As she stepped outside her hut, she instantly sensed that something was not right. There was a shift in the atmosphere, she felt a strong dark presence. A witch or a wizard. Either way it was someone with magical powers greater than hers.

Ma'Dika was in a state of alert. She lifted her head and paid closer attention to the atmosphere. Her ear popped and she heard as if from a distance a familiar sound in the world of African witches: the Okerekere.

In an instant her all seeing eye opened and she saw him coming towards her enveloped in a cloud of dust and smoke. Yes! It was him, the famous jester and drum playing Nwanshi dwarf who usually preceded the entrance of Funke, the Great Nigerian sorceress, queen of all African witches. Dressed in nothing but rags around his waist with his face covered in white chalk The Okerekere was frantically beating his drum whilst dancing and doing all sorts of acrobatics.

The sound of the drums got louder and abruptly ceased

when he entered Ma'Dika compounds. The Okerere silently knelt down. Suddenly a whirlwind of sand lifted up from the ground like a volcanic eruption and there she was; Funke, the Great Nigerian sorceress, queen of all African witches.

She was over six feet tall, wearing a long multi-coloured rag dress made of handwoven Nigerian akwete cloth. On her feet she wore ankle bracelets made of white shells and her face was covered by a brown and red Yoruba tribal mask. Rumour has it that behind the mask Funke had one of the most beautiful faces ever seen in the whole of Africa.

Head bowed down in the presence of Funke, Ma'Dika was puzzled. What could have brought the mighty Funke to a lower ranked witch's abode? As matter of fact, Ma'Dika recalls that at the last African witches convention, Funke dared not acknowledge her presence and treated her like a subservient. So why was she here?

"Your highness," saluted Ma'Dika. She continued, "How can your humble servant be of service?"

Funke looked down on her and said from behind her mask, "Ma'Dika, witch from the baobab land, what is happening in your land?"

What was the meaning of the question? thought Ma'Dika. Not sure if this was a trick question or not. After a moment of hesitation, she replied, "There is peace in the land of the baobab tree, your highness."

"You fool!" roared Funke. Ma'Dika was startled.

"Sorry your highness, I don't understand," stuttered Ma'Dika.

Funke looked up and began to prophesy; "Like twin sisters from the same womb, glory and disgrace are heading towards us hand in hand. While you eat, sleep and drink, a friend and foe has arisen upon the underworld. And you, witch of the land of the baobab destiny has chosen you as a warrior in this battle."

"Me?" asked Ma'Dika, "I am one of the youngest and least experienced witches, how can I play a role that would impact the underworld?"

Funke disclosed to Ma'Dika that at the convention of the world's queen witches there was a divination that a star like no other had appeared in the skies. Once every one hundred years a star enters the world with a mantel to shake the underworld in its core. This time around, that star will be through Africa.

"A star?" asked Ma'Dika.

"Yes," replied Funke, "a girl born from the Sakola Tribe, it is she."

"Wait a minute,' said Ma'Dika. "I am the spiritual guide for this tribe. I initiate and coronate all its chiefs."

"Foolish witch, finally catching up?" grinned Funke.

Not quite, thought Ma'Dika, besides there was no need for insults. But she dared not voice her thoughts aloud. So she chose a more diplomatic way of responding to Funke; "Well, I see the connection, but not quite clear on the role I have to play."

"Richard Sakola's daughter's star is powerful enough to make her an ally or an enemy of the underworld. To escape a lurking doom before she reaches her time of wisdom, this child must be initiated into the underworld by being crowned chief of Sakola tribe and betrothed to king Abaddon as wife."

"Chief of Tribe Sakola? But this position is reserved to Sam, Richard Sakola's first born son," claimed Ma'Dika.

Funke barked, "Silence! The danger is so great there is a need to unite forces. The girl child belongs to a powerful Nigerian bloodline through her mother Oluchi. The position of chief of tribe would create a coalition between occult forces in both Nigeria and Congo and give her greater authority than Sakola's son."

In passing, she added, "This alliance would elevate your position amongst the African sorceresses federation."

Ma'Dika liked the sound of that. Finally, she will acquire status and respect. She still had one question; "I think it's an immense honour, oh queen sorceress, to facilitate one of our great Lord Abaddon marriages, but what is the objective of this union?"

"Our ancestors say there is no greater bond than that of marriage. A union with the great Lord Abaddon would seal this child's fate in the underworld forever!"

"I see now," whispered Ma'Dika, her face still prostrated before Funke.

Funke pointed her index finger in the direction of Ma'Dika and conjured, "I have spoken! Now witch from the baobab land do what must be done to secure the integrity of our world! If you succeed, you will be second only to me in the whole of Africa. But woe unto you if you fail."

"Yes your highness, I will not let you down," swore Ma'Dika.

In a violent whirlwind, Funke instantly vanished from Ma'Dika's sight. The okerekere resumed his drum beats as he slowly walked away from Ma'Dika, disappearing in a cloud of dust and smoke in the same manner he had appeared.

This meeting between Funke and Ma'Dika took place twenty-six years ago, on the day of Angelique's birth.

ISABELLE KAMALANDWA BRYAN

Chapter 5
Angelique Meets Ma'Dika

At about noon time, the limousine arrived at the family villa in the exclusive district of Mount Ngaliema. All Angelique wanted was to get into her bikini and take a dip in their imposing Roman-style swimming pool, then retire in her room. Swimming would help her calm down and at the same time, refresh her in this extremely hot and humid African climate, which she was no longer accustomed to. She was barely in her second lap when Oluchi appeared out of the house and headed for the pool patio area.

"Angelique, come here, darling," she called out whilst settling herself down on one of the white and beige pool sofas. She was quickly followed by Mousa, their faithful house help, who carried a tray with a jug of lime-flavoured orange juice and a couple of large glasses, which he placed on the table by Oluchi's side.

Angelique was in no frame of mind for conversations, but because it was her mum and to avoid being branded rude, she reluctantly stepped out of the pool, wrapped her toned coca-cola shaped figure in a large towel and joined Oluchi. She sank by the side of her mother, who served a glass of juice and handed it to her.

"Thanks, mum," she mumbled as she took the juice and sipped it slowly, staring off into space.

Oluchi had not yet changed out of her black funeral African wrap. The loss of Richard had taken a toll on her and she looked older than her fifty-four years of age. She tenderly placed a hand on her daughter's shoulder and said, "Sweetheart, I know you are still processing what has happened. But for us life continues and there are some very important matters we need to discuss."

"Can it not wait?"

"No, it can't. Your dad charged me with making sure you carry on his legacy as the next tribal chief."

Angelique relived the flash in her dream about her father bowing to her.

"That's fine," she agreed. Her understanding was that these traditional practices were purely symbolic and she was happy to become the next chief to honour her father's memory.

"Good! Now there is something you must do."

"Like what?"

"You need to see Ma'Dika. She is the one who initiated your father, and she'll need to initiate you too."

"Ma'Dika..." repeated Angelique pensively. That's the name her father mentioned in the dream.

"Who is she? And what does the initiation involve?" she questioned.

"She is the Wise One and I don't know what the initiation process involves. I am a foreigner in this land, remember? But all I know is that your coronation needs to take place seven days from today."

Angelique sighed. That was an unexpected disturbance in her life. "Fine, I'll go see her when I have time."

"Unfortunately, that is not possible; you must see her after the burial, which means today. Sorry, but that's tradition."

"Mum, this tradition is whack. Who cares about tribal chiefs in the 21st century? We are not in the stone ages. I am tired, I need to rest."

"Don't be childish, you know these instructions were left by your father. It's very important that you do what you are told."

Without a word, Angelique dropped her towel, headed back to the pool and took a long and deep dive into the clear blue chlorine water under Oluchi's startled glare.

Angelique was not the least superstitious and did not believe in God or any higher beings for that matter. Her dad was an intelligent, educated man; therefore, it greatly disappointed her that he allowed himself to be hauled in these meaningless ancestral practices. She, on the contrary, had little tolerance for African traditional beliefs.

A bunch of archaic mambo jambo as far as she was concerned. However, even she was forced to acknowledge that there was something surreal and unexplainable about the recurring dream she had about Richard prior to his death. Especially considering that the first time she heard of Ma'Dika's name was in that vision of the night, long before the conversation with her mother. Therefore, regardless of her views on her ancestors' practices, she dared not disregard her dad's dying wish.

The drive through the countryside en route to the Mutambu village from the capital turned out to be a delightful experience. Angelique took great pleasure in admiring the equatorial nation's rainforest vegetation, which was a sharp contrast to the much softer British landscape. She was fascinated by the diverging practices too. For instance, the sophisticated and modern 'welcome break' services on UK motorways Angelique was used to seeing were replaced here with happy villagers displaying their local produce by the dusty roadside to sell to motorists. On sale were local specialities, which ranged from exotic fruits and vegetables to roasted crickets and bush meat. The prices were such a bargain that Angelique could not resist asking the driver to stop over to purchase some custard apple fruits, tamarinds and mangosteens.

They reached Mutambu village after a journey of approximately two hours. Ma'Dika's dwelling was situated in the village's outskirts, four hundred metres inside an enormous plain surrounded by long green grass, sparse acacia trees and one baobab tree.

"Here we are, madam," announced the chauffeur. "Unfortunately, we cannot go any further; the witch doctor's house is that hut in the middle of the field."

Angelique stepped out of the grey E-Class Mercedes and beheld the African Savanna in its splendour. The panorama extended as far as her eyes could see. The sun slowly sunk west as a gentle cool evening breeze swayed the tall grass, slowly rocking them to sleep. The multi-coloured butterflies put up their last flying performance of the day in the sky, as if in Angelique's honour, to the sound of happy chirping field crickets. It was breath-taking.

She turned to the driver and said, "Please wait for me," as she set off.

"Of course, madam."

Although the scenery was beautiful, accessing the hut was a pain in the real sense of the term. Angelique had to battle through the shrubs; it took her a good ten minutes to arrive at the destination, all the while wishing she had worn more comfortable shoes. Her black stiletto definitely was a major contributor to her discomfort.

She had barely reached the doorstep when the small wooden door opened and an old lady dressed in black from head to toe came out. She was only about four feet tall and not easy on the eye, to say the least. She had a black scarf on her head and her face was covered with incisions of strange symbols that only she knew the meanings of. Her skin was as black as charcoal. There she was, Ma'Dika, the witch doctor known in the tribal language as 'Nganga Nkisi'.

She smiled at the sight of Angelique, who nervously smiled back, noticing that she only had about five yellow teeth in her mouth.

"Angelique, I am happy to meet you, finally," she said with a crackling voice. "Your father was a great Chief." She put her arms around Angelique and hugged her. Ma'Dika reeked of a mixture of sweat and old damp rusty furniture. Angelique fought the urge to push her away and run straight back to the car. As if she had read her thoughts, Ma'Dika reassured Angelique, patting her on the cheek. "Everything will be well; you don't have to worry. You'll need to spend three days here with me."

"Excuse me? I beg your pardon?" Angelique's eyeballs were about to pop out of their sockets in disbelief.

She nodded. "Yes, the initiation will take three days. I will release you after it is completed and you will come back to the village with your family for the coronation on Sunday."

Someone was playing a bad joke on her. Angelique made up her mind that there was no way she was staying in the middle of nowhere with a smelly old lady. She doubted that the shack even had sanitary facilities.

"Sorry, but I am a very busy woman. I cannot just spend three whole days here. I have pressing business to attend to back in England. Can the initiation be shortened to an hour?"

Ma'Dika looked Angelique straight in the eyes. Her eyes turned fiery red, which sent a cold chill down Angelique's spine. Her bravado vanished as fast as a gold digger dumps a broke partner.

Ma'Dika scolded her; "Rule number one, you do not lie to me. There is no pressing business. I have an all-seeing eye. Rule number two, you do not disobey me. I have the power to unlock the known. The greater the destiny, the greater the price to pay! Now come inside!"

"Yes, ma'am," Angelique was shaken and just plain scared. She scratched her head like a little girl and requested that Ma'Dika give her a minute to call the chauffeur to inform him that he did not need to wait for her and instruct him to come back for her in three days. Her request was granted.

She was uncertain whether to cry, laugh hysterically or slap herself in the face to check she wasn't having a nightmare. More extraordinarily, it baffled her that she was bullied by a four-foot old lady with only five teeth in her mouth.

As Ma'Dika disappeared inside the hut, Angelique took out her cell phone from her bag to call the driver muttering under her breath, "What the heck…"

ISABELLE KAMALANDWA BRYAN

Chapter 6
The Initiation

Ma'Dika's hut was cone-like in shape made from reddish-brown mud. The roofing was a traditional thatched grass known as mandala in their dialect, which consisted of weaved leaves from a coconut plant. The interior of the hut comprised one large space used both as a living room and bedroom. It reposed on unevenly laid concrete. The premises lacked water and electricity supply. For lighting Ma'Dika used a couple of old design petrol lamps and a villager delivered drinking water fetched daily from the village water pump. Ma'Dika used the clear water stream situated only a quarter of a mile away to bathe and wash clothes, though Angelique doubted she made that trip often. The only furniture in the house were a couple of straw mats and four basic indigenous stools made from wood.

The cooking area was located at the back of the house on the right hand side and on the far left a latrine concealed behind a fence of growing bushes.

Village residents had a tendency to be self-sufficient. For instance, Ma'Dika kept some chickens, ducks and a few goats which provided her with a supply of fresh eggs and milk. She also cultivated vegetables and herbs she used in her traditional herbal remedies.

The fact that someone would live in such appalling conditions in the twenty-first century disconcerted Angelique. She had serious concerns about contracting some type of tropical infection or virus in this unsanitary prehistoric environment. There were some necessary items that automatically came to her mind which by the looks of things Ma'Dika had not heard of: toilet paper, toothpaste, shampoo, moisturisers, a bed to name but a few. On the upside, she had her phone with her, Angelique thought. Should she find herself unable to support the living conditions she'd ring her mum who would send the chauffeur to collect her. She congratulated herself for having braid extensions, her beloved weaves would have been tricky to manage and have ended up all tangled in this humidity.

Ma'Dika wasted no time in kicking off with the initiation ritual. She ordered Angelique to take off her classy two-piece trousers and jacket suit and handed her a large African loincloth to wear and rubbed palm oil all over her body. She dipped her index finger in what looked like grounded chalk and drew signs and symbols on Angelique's face, arms and feet. She later twisted the neck of a white rooster and gave Angelique its boiled flesh mixed with unfamiliar herbs to eat. At the first mouthful of the slimy pale green stew Angelique fought the combined urges to throw up and pass out. Sadly for her, Ma'Dika gave her no other choice than to polish off the large wood bowl, which she managed to do with great difficulty. Instead of water, Ma'Dika served Angelique a green tart liquid concoction which went straight to her head and unsettled her stomach. By now Angelique was convinced that she was going to die at the hands of this mad woman like a poor dog and details of her death will spread across TripAdvisor sites as a case study about the do's and don'ts when one travels to Congo. She contemplated escaping before it was too late, but had no strength, her legs had turned to jelly.

Ma'Dika proceeded to blow tobacco smoke in her face while chanting and making incantations. Angelique felt her body fall to the ground and her spirit slip into a state of semi-consciousness caught between this world and the next, between reality and fantasy, in a limbo. It was in this grey and black nebulous atmosphere that her ears and eyes opened. She perceived a man who had the appearance of a higher being. He spoke and declared that she was chosen from her brethren and all maidens in the African continent for greatness and dominion.

He took Angelique by the hand to a field gorging with sheep and goats. Each animal had its full name written on its back. Some had their little ones that had names on them too. There was no animal that did not have a name. The herd had the names of every member of Angelique's family including those she had never met before.

At the sight of the higher being, the flock gathered together. One section of the animals formed a base, the others started positioning themselves one on top of the other until they had formed a perfect six-tier pyramid. Angelique noted that all the animals were extremely docile apart from one that bore the name of Sam Sakola which put up some resistance. However, he could not resist the authority of the higher being and eventually fell in line.

"Now Angelique Sakola, go up!" the higher being ordered.

Angelique obeyed and climbed the goat and sheep made mountain and steadily reached the tip. Once at the top she got slightly scared because the mountain was extremely high. The higher being proclaimed "subdue and rule Angelique Sakola!"

Suddenly a violent easterly wind blew in Angelique's direction forcing her to cover her eyes with her hand and crouch down to maintain her balance. As the wind ceased, the scene equally changed and when she opened her eyes, to her amazement she was in Ma'Dika's courtyard holding the same crouched position, whilst the latter chanted and frantically gyrated in front of Angelique.

Moments later, when Angelique sought the meaning of her experience, the witch doctor explained that the sheep and goats represented the people in her tribe whose luck she would hog in order to attain great heights. Angelique expressed serious misgivings on the idea of dispossessing her mother and sisters, prompting Ma'Dika to elaborate further on the reason.

"Such is the law of greatness," she said. "Only one can be brought into the limelight out of every thousands and the rest must remain in the shadows to make it possible. For that purpose tradition demands that you become the provider for your bloodline. Their wellbeing now lies in your hands, in the same way it did in your father's. Even though they are destined to underachieve, they'll rely on you to provide for them. That's the law."

It did not sound so bad after Ma'Dika's clarification. Angelique vowed to give nothing but the best to all her relatives.

SAKOLA

Chapter 7
A Trip to Metropolis

It was about midnight, Angelique laid in the dark on the hard uncomfortable straw mat by MaDika's side, staring at a ceiling made of grass wondering what would happen if it started to rain.

She was struggling to go to sleep, still reeling over earlier events and having to contend with Ma'Dika's extremely loud snoring. The afternoon session with the witch doctor was the most bizarre experience she had ever gone through. It caused her to recall African folklore stories she was told by their housemaids in her childhood. Maybe there were not mere tales after all.

Savanna temperatures during the rainy season were usually cooler at night, which suited Angelique's metabolism and helped her unwind. Therefore, after about a good hour of tossing and turning, the resounding snoring of Ma'Dika turned into a distant out of tune symphony as Angelique finally dozed off. Her eyes had been shut for what seemed like only ten minutes when she felt a hand shake her shoulder. A beautiful young Apache Indian girl dressed in a native Cheyenne buckskin dress with a hawk feather headdress holding her lustrous long black hair was standing beside the straw mat. Arms folded she gazed at Angelique with amusement.

"You took your time to go to sleep," she whinged.

Angelique was bemused, wondering who the girl was and how she got there. She would have strayed a long way from her homeland.

"Get up Angelique, we have work to do. I don't have all night," she said, clapping her hands.

Angelique stared at her trying to make sense of what was going on. The young girl stared back at her. It was then, Angelique recognised the fiery red eyes of Ma'Dika. It dawned on her that this young Apache Indian girl was actually Ma'Dika.

"Ma'Dika? Is that you?" she queried.

"Bingo! Come on, we have a lot to do," Ma'Dika whispered. "Follow me!"

Angelique swiftly jumped up and followed Ma'Dika. Rapidly she noticed that the setting was different. The inside of the hut looked prettier, colourful in an eerie kind of way. It had transformed into an enchanted Brothers Grimm African-type maisonette. Although she tread on the heels of Ma'Dika, Angelique's feet were not touching the ground, she had a sensation of floating rather than walking. By pure instinct, she turned back to glance at where she laid and to her shocking horror her body was still lying on the straw mat and so was Ma'Dika's! Angelique gasped, then screamed.

Ma'Dika laughed, "Welcome to your first lesson; astral projection."

In the astral sphere, the world was seen through the lens of mysticism. One night in the physical world was like thirty nights in the underworld. Angelique discovered that she could fly, and pretty fast too. That night Ma'Dika took Angelique on a tour of the celestial sphere, to visit the zodiac constellations that make a ring around the earth. The witch doctor taught Angelique about modern horoscopic astrology which are the twelve signs of the horoscope and the classical elements they are associated with: fire, air, earth and water. Angelique received wisdom to read and interpret the signs as well as manipulate the elements in order to control circumstances around her and make them work in her favour and against her enemies. Ma'Dika introduced Angelique to Funke who trained in ancient African occultism and voodoo. Funke gifted Angelique her own customised tribal mask made of bronze.

Angelique mastered the art of black and white magic. From the top of a snowy mountain in the North Pole, under Ma'Dika's tutorship and the watchful eyes of the hawk spirit, Angelique acquired the knowledge to make incantations, practised casting spells and summoning spirits from the air and from the underworld. She became skilful at initiating astral projection and altering her shape. By the end of the session, Angelique was able to transform into most animals or birds of her choice, including human beings.

At about four a.m. the following day, they flew back from Alaska and landed in the plain in front of a baobab tree. Angelique noted the tree looked familiar, as matter of fact, very similar to the one her father disappeared into in her dream.

As she pondered on that thought, Ma'Dika knocked on the tree three times and recited a magic formula, "To the three inverted libwa make way for the African sorceress."

The tree opened to a tunnel, Ma'Dika led the way followed by Angelique. Inside the tunnel was a flight of stairs that went all the way down into the centre of the earth. At the bottom of the stair was a wooden door with the following inscription, "Welcome to the underworld, domain of Abaddon, king of the bottomless pit."

Behind the door stood a bustling Metropolis. It reminded Angelique of a comic book futuristic city. The atmosphere was foggy and grey. There was no sunlight, because the sun did not shine in the underworld. As a substitute a couple of moon-like satellites provided some faint light to the city. Angelique noticed there were houses, buildings, factories releasing sulphur smoke in the air, cars, flying saucers, shops, businesses, people and other kinds of beings which Ma'Dika explained were spirits. Those spirits came in different shapes and sizes. Some looked human, some looked like animals, some like a cross between humans and animals, some were just hideous monsters. They each went about their business.

Nobody seemed bothered by the presence of Angelique and Ma'Dika. Angelique was curious to know why humans would live in this world. Ma'Dika informed her that the only people who had the right to enter the underworld were confirmed witches and wizards. In the first instance, some would have made the choice to live there and only visit the outside world on assignments or to run errands. She was aware of many who had settled in the Metropolis and had families. In the second instance, were those who would visit the city only on missions, such was their case. Finally, in the third instance, were those brought into that realm as slaves to serve Abaddon, the ruler of the underworld.

Ma'Dika's discourse left Angelique with a burning question.

"Ma'Dika, does this mean I am a witch?" she queried.

"What do you think?" Ma'Dika quizzed back with a wink.

Angelique thought about it for a minute, was she? Wasn't she? Oh crap!

"Come on, we need to get you registered, before you get in trouble," said Ma'Dika. Angelique was not sure what Ma'Dika meant. Why should she be in trouble?

Ma'Dika tapped on the ground with her feet three and half times and suddenly a passport control cabin surged from the ground. Inside sat a bald man. He had no race and was every race. Dressed in an all-black police officer type uniform, he was muscular and wore heavy, dark sunglasses, which, by the way, Angelique thought was ridiculous, there was no sun in that god forsaken place. The man had a badge on which read, the immigration officer.

His eyes glued on this computer screen, with a grave voice he asked Ma'Dika, "Name of your visitor?"

"Angelique Sakola," Ma'Dika replied.

He began typing on his computer keyboard as he continued with his questioning.

"Purpose for the visit?"

"Initiation."

"Number of entries?"

"Unlimited."

"Name of sponsor?"

"Chief Abaddon."

The immigration officer paused for a while as he ran a check on his computer database. Finally, after about five minutes, he lifted up his head and said, "All clear!" As Angelique assumed that this process was over, the immigration officer ordered her to come forward. A hesitant Angelique was encouraged by the nod from Ma'Dika to walk towards the immigration officer.

"Stretch forward your left hand, and place it on top of the desk," he ordered. Angelique obeyed. He held her hand, picked up a wooden stamp machine from under his desk and pressed it firmly against Angelique's inside wrist. The end result was a transparent barcode which Angelique struggled to decipher.

Letting go of Angelique's hand the immigration officer said with a ceremonious voice "Angelique Sakola, your request for citizenship of the great underworld kingdom has been approved. You are free to come and go as you please in all territories of the underworld. Whenever pressed gently with your thumb this invisible barcode will transport you to the mystical and magical world. This is your only access to the underworld and its mystical powers."

He handed out to her an instruction leaflet while he continued, "The barcode is invisible to the naked eye, but it releases a glow that is visible to agents of the underworld. However, it is very susceptible to extreme light. Take good care of it and welcome to the underworld!"

Following these words, the immigration officer and the passport control cabin disappeared back into the ground.

Angelique understood that even in the underworld there was such a thing as border control. Ma'Dika explained if anyone attempted to enter the underworld without going through the immigration officer they would get arrested and trapped in the underworld forever while their body in the physical world gets eaten by worms. This has happened in many cases where humans would self-initiate, usually through books, without guidance from an underworld agent.

Once all formalities were completed, they hopped onto a floating taxi which dropped them at the gate of a factory. Its name was 'The Transit Slave Factory'. Once inside, Ma'Dika signed in her and Angelique on the register at the reception desk. The receptionist, a half-human half-goat creature, unlocked a large cast iron door which opened to an immense dungeon where men and women chained to a giant capstan were made to grind it day and night nonstop. They produced energy designed to power the invisible engine of the underworld. Dressed in dirty rags they appeared to be in excruciating pain, which was accentuated by the harsh whips inflicted on them by the beastly looking guards. There was a smell – despair, fear and sweat – that emanated from the prison. As Angelique looked intensely at these suffering men and women, she spotted her father among the slaves.

"Dad!"

Richard lifted up his eyes and recognised his daughter, "Angelique ma chérie!"

Angelique ran into the arms of her father. With a hand gesture Ma'Dika commanded the guards not to stop Angelique from embracing her father. Angelique held on tight to Richard, "Dad, Oh my God, I never thought I'd see you again. I missed you. What are you doing here?"

"I miss you too. That was part of my contract ma chérie. I agreed to dedicate some of my remaining years to the underworld. I trust Ma'Dika will give you more details."

Later on Ma'Dika explained to Angelique that although to the outside world her father had died, according to the laws of the universe, it was not yet his time to pass because he had not used up the years which were allocated to him on earth. People in the underworld such as Angelique's father could trade some of their years in exchange for power and wealth on earth. The traded years are the ones spent in the underworld as slaves. In Richard's case he traded his remaining years for his daughter's fortune.

"Time to go, Angelique," urged Ma'Dika.

With tears in her eyes Angelique squeezed her father's hand tightly, "Will I see you again?"

"I have permission to attend your consecration so you'll see me again," replied Richard. Letting go of his daughter, he placed his hand back on the lever and resumed grinding. It was five in the morning when they both returned to their bodies. Angelique was buzzing from the mysteries she had learnt, but the pivotal point was seeing her father again. She was moved that her father would sacrifice his years for her success. She vowed to herself to find a way not only to go back to visit him, but figure out how to set him free.Thus, she made the decision to be the best apprentice Ma'Dika had ever had. She promised herself to make a concerted effort in learning hard and become the best in her craft.

ISABELLE KAMALANDWA BRYAN

Chapter 8
The Godparents: Amazonia and Mammon

"Wake up Angelique!" There was a middle-aged English man with blond hair and blue eyes standing by the mat. He wore a grey pin-stripe suit and a black English bowler hat.

A quick look in his fiery red eyes, Angelique discerned that it was Ma'Dika in a different body. She chuckled within herself, this old lady was far from dull, her playfulness was quite entertaining.

"Tonight, we are going to meet your Godmother," Ma'Dika announced.

That sounded exciting to Angelique. She had a Godmother! They both flew away from their bodies and in no time arrived by the shores of the Amazon River in Brazil. Hidden deep in the rainforest, the river was a scintillating clear green, softly lit up by the astral half moon. The night was clear and mystical, multi-coloured fluorescent damselflies and dragonflies silently fluttered over the water.

Ma'Dika lifted her hands by the shore and sanctimoniously made an invocation, "I Ma'Dika sorceress from the land of the great baobab summon you, spirit of the waters, lady of the lake, queen Amazonia, come to us."

Upon hearing her summon, the river began to agitate and bubble, causing the dragonflies and damselflies to scatter. Heads of exceptionally beautiful female creatures with remarkably long hair started emerging on the surface of the water. Through the limpid water Angelique noticed instead of feet they had green and orange coloured fish tails. She could not believe her eyes, so mermaids did exist.

They came in every different skin colour known to man, one as stunning as the next. Although they were endowed with extraordinary beauty, Angelique noted that they all had extremely pale eyes which gave them a sinister look even when they smiled. They formed a circle, and a mermaid emerged from the middle of the ring. If that was at all possible, she was even more striking than the ones around her, the most beautiful woman Angelique had ever seen. She arose to the surface from underneath with the water up to her waist. Her long green hair fell from her shoulders, covering her breasts all the way down, merging with the scintillating green water in perfect harmony. She had long lashes and very pale green eyes. Her skin was fair and had a mesmerising glow. She sported a green, purple and gold fishtail. On her head was a golden crown encrusted with rubies and emeralds. Her presence was hypnotising. She was Amazonia the queen of the sirens.

With an echoing voice, Queen Amazonia spoke, "Ma'Dika from the land of the great baobab. Why do you disturb my peace? What brings you to the magical waters of the Amazon?"

Ma'Dika replied, "Oh! Great queen of the lake, it was revealed in the prophecy of the stars that the next ruler of the financial world and wife of Lord Abaddon will come from the land of the great baobab. Angelique Sakola is the chosen one to reign and rule for one and a third of a season. As the perpetual Godmother of Lord Abaddon's brides I have brought her here for the water ritual as the symbol of unity between the underworld and the water world."

Amazonia nodded in guise of approval, opened her arms wide and called Angelique to her, "Come to me Angelique."

Slightly hesitant and fascinated simultaneously, Angelique set foot in the water and walked toward Amazonia. The mermaids opened up the circle to let her through, their fishtails swaying softly under the transparent green water. Angelique walked into the water until she was but a few metres from Amazonia utterly mesmerized by her aura. Although the water was at both their waist level, Amazonia was twice the size of Angelique. She plunged her hand inside the river, brought out a bracelet with large round crystals which she gave to Angelique. "This bracelet will be your protection and symbol of alliance with all the water spirits that reign in the universe from the Mamiwatas from the river Zaire to the queen mother kingdom in the Atlantic Ocean. This covenant cannot be broken!"

Angelique took the bracelet and put it around her wrist. It was shining and had green and red reflections. It was lovely. In return, she was made to take an oath of perpetual allegiance to the water spirits. The mermaids offered her many more jewelleries with precious stones and played with her in the water.

While splashing with the mermaids, she caught a reflection of herself in the water. She'd always described herself as a good looking girl, above average, but had no recollection of ever looking so fabulous. She barely recognised herself. She was as beautiful as the sirens. Her naturally medium-size afro hair had converted into extremely long black and white afro with soft curls. Her skin was intensely smooth as if it had been photoshopped. Angelique absolutely loved the way she looked in the astral world.

The sirens styled her hair playfully and adorned it with a crown of shells and amazon lilies. She felt an intense, exhilarating sensation being in their company. However, a nagging feeling was birthed in her when Ma'Dika made a reference to her as the bride of Abaddon.

She had plans to obtain further clarification from her on that issue once they were back from the astral trip. Nevertheless, overall Angelique was really enjoying her introduction to the spirit world, even though Ma'Dika was quick to put an end to the fun by whisking Angelique away from the sirens. They had another journey ahead that night, to London, England.

Angelique's curiosity was aroused as they drew closer to the iconic Tower of London, "Why are we in London?"

"You're going to meet your Godfather."

"I am getting a Godfather too? Wow!"

They landed at the gates of the gothic London Bridge cathedral and walked in through the main entrance under the intimidating glares and grunts of the two residents' winged dragon gargoyles. They had red fiery eyes and they would intermittently spit fire in the air.

Ma'Dika and Angelique made their way through the cathedral's internal street to the main hall known as the sanctuary room. The hall which boasted a medieval stained glass surround was divided in three parts: the congregation area where there were chairs for the worshippers; the choir zone, known as the ministers area; and the bishop's throne backed by the saints' screen, which consisted of one hundred and fifty clay carved statues of departed saints. The entire hall was lit up with candles placed along the aisles. Ma'Dika followed by Angelique made her way to the bishop's throne, where she stopped facing the saints' screen. Above the figures of the saints laid a row of thirteen golden carved four-winged dragons. Two of their wings were positioned asymmetrically along their bodies and the other two were lifted up toward the golden graven image of a man standing on a pile of gold bullions. The figure of the man was about ten feet tall, dressed in a long robe covering his feet. He had an abnormally pointed nose and no hair.

Ma'Dika approached the Bishop's throne and lit up the large red candle placed on the pulpit and as soon as it started burning, the atmosphere went through a sudden metamorphosis. The statutes of the saints came to life and their eyes opened. Some turned their heads to their counterparts and started chatting and others stared straight at both women inquisitively. The winged dragons flapped their wings and spitted fire. The room was filled with chatter. Ma'Dika placed both hands on the burning red candle and conjured in Latin, "Veni Spiritus mammona, vocat spiritus niger pythonissam mammona."

It sounded like gibberish to Angelique, but once the conjuration was completed the golden statue of the man standing on the gold bullion came to life too. He floated toward Ma'Dika and Angelique and addressed them with a calm and cool voice, while the saints and the dragons watched on, "Sorceress from the land of the baobab, why have you come to disturb me?"

Ma'Dika bowed before him, "Lord Mammon, I have brought your Goddaughter Angelique Sakola, destined to shine in the financial world and future bride of our king Abaddon for your commendation." Mammon turned to Angelique, trailed by the glares of all the saints and the winged dragons. "There she is, my next protégée, Angelique," he said with a sharp hissy tone in his voice.

Ma'Dika introduced him to Angelique, "Meet Mammon, the Lord of riches and ruler of wealth, your Godfather."

Angelique bowed to him. He lifted her chin with one finger, which had an extraordinary long nail and stared at her intensely with his silver eyes. He was shining gold from head to toe and apparently held the key to the wealth of most of the world's richest men. Very few people, according to Ma'Dika, could reach the highest echelon of success and power in the world without making a covenant with lord Mammon first. He had the power to grant wealth and knowledge to acquire it.

"I've heard a lot about you Angelique. The Sakola name has come from obscurity to notoriety," he said. "Our Master Abaddon has got great plans for you."

Twice now reference had been made about Abaddon as her future groom, and that was starting to alarm

Angelique. Events were taking a turn she was not comfortable with and was unsure she could control. What on earth was she getting into?

Mammon placed a rusty gold coin in the palm of her hand. He whistled and one of the dragons brought over an envelope to him, which he handed over to Angelique.

"This is the offer of appointment that you need to sign," he said. Inside the envelope was a rusted gold coin and a dusty letter that described her post, remuneration and benefits. The thirteen-page document stipulated that the named Angelique Sakola would be appointed as the next CEO of WAXXA, the largest bank in the world. Very few people would have heard of WAXXA and those who have, had little or no information about it. Unbeknown to many WAXXA was the bank of all banks, or in other words the godmother of all banks in the physical. Although extremely discreet in its operations WAXXA controlled every single bank and financial institution in the physical world.

The contract guaranteed Angelique's financial security on the proviso she served and vowed a lifetime allegiance to the underworld. The document also contained the terms and conditions in such small prints that reading them would have required the assistance of magnifying glasses. Angelique did not bother to go through them.

Then, Mammon took out a small dagger and pricked Angelique's index finger. "This type of contract can only be signed with blood," he said, with a crackling voice inviting her to stamp the dusty letter.

He was offering her the world on a silver plate. She was

tempted yet still unsure about the wedding reference. She gradually pulled her finger away and begged Mammon to be excused as she took Ma'Dika to one side.

"What are you doing Angelique?" Ma'Dika asked whispering wondering what on earth this girl was up to.

"All this sounds amazing, but what's the wedding to Abaddon all about? I have a boyfriend and I like him."

Ma'Dika scoffed at Angelique, "Foolish girl, it's a spiritual marriage, a mere formality. You'll still be able to have normal relationships in the physical world."

"So it won't interfere with my love life?"

"No it won't, I promise! Now let's not make Mammon wait. This is an opportunity of a lifetime." Ma'Dika ushered Angelique back to Mammon.

Squeezing drops of blood from the incision made by Mammon, Angelique signed the contract haunted by an ubiquitous premonition that it was her soul she had signed away.

Mammon took the contract, placed it on the bishop pulpit, poured wax off the red candle that Ma'Dika had lit up and affixed the underworld seal on it.

He then raised his hands and proclaimed in latin, "tenebris regnat in saecula saeculorum."

The saints echoed his words by chanting "Vivat Abaddon!" The winged dragons blew hot fire out of their mouths. Finally, he levitated further above the ground and before regaining his carved posture he praised Angelique on making what he referred to as the best decision anyone could make and guaranteed a prosperous future awaited her.

And then he warned her that under no circumstances could the contract be broken. Any attempt to do so will trigger the penalty of death. These were his final words as he, the saints and the winged dragons re-adopted their inert state. The commotion that had saturated the sanctuary room vanished. The candles stopped burning. It was time to leave.

If there were ever grey areas in her beliefs about the supernatural, those were now non-existent. There was no longer any doubt in Angelique's mind that entities more powerful than human beings existed.

On the one hand, she felt special she was chosen to lead such a great and exciting life. On the other, the creepiest part of her experience was the signing of the contract with blood. As she lay on the mat next to a snoring Ma'Dika in the early hours of the morning, Mammon's last words resonated in her head like a repetitive track, "This contract cannot be broken!"

"Oh crap! What have I gotten myself into?" She began to wonder. Maybe she should have made an effort to read the small print. It was too late.

ISABELLE KAMALANDWA BRYAN

Chapter 9
Family Feud

Their heads were barely down when Ma'Dika's and Angelique's sleep was cut short by the angry voice of a shouting man outside the hut.

"Ma'Dika, you evil witch! Backstabber! I know Angelique's inside with you. Bring her out!"

It was Sam, Angelique's half brother. With his fists clinched in fury, he was standing about twenty metres from the hut seething with rage. Dressed in a worn-out used-to-be white shirt, a pair of jeans and trainers, he relentlessly threw out a wave of obscenities until Ma'Dika emerged from the shack followed by Angelique.

"I knew it!" yelled Sam as he saw Angelique. "You have initiated her as the chief of the tribe, you betrayed me!"

"Don't you dare speak to me in that tone!" retorted Ma'Dika "There was no guarantee that you were going to be the next chief."

"Yes, you told my mother it would be so, you lying old hag. I have been robbed! I am the first male, tradition demands that I be crowned the next chief."

"Watch your mouth Sam! The first born was not crowned because the spirit world chose a woman to represent the tribe! So now be gone!"

Fully aware she was shattering Sam's dream, Ma'Dika stood up to Sam anyway. Rarely in her profession was any situation straightforward. Masking truths and making U-turns were vital skills needed if one aspired to be a powerful witch. And she had mastered both arts, hence why she was now one of the most powerful witches thanks to the deal she had made with Funke. She was no longer a nobody, she was feared by her peers.

Humans were by nature gullible and weak, willing to embrace anything that bore the promise of glory, without fully weighing the repercussions Ma'Dika thought. The same applied to Angelique, who was under the illusion that she would have a normal love life after marrying Abaddon. Can anyone be married and their life remain the same? Can married and single really walk together? She had fallen into temptation, the perfect bait that ensnared and blinded common sense.

And Sam, he was the unlucky casualty of a U-turn. It was true that he was in line to succeed Richard as the next chief of tribe. He was even initiated into the arts of dark magic. Sadly, he would be confined to the role of a second-rate wizard as Angelique steps in as the new chief. The stakes were far too high to fret over breaking the promise made to Sam and crowning the first woman as chief of tribe. Ma'Dika empathised with Sam's disappointment; nevertheless had no regrets about the decision made.

Sam, on the other hand, was not prepared to go down without a fight. Far from it. "Fine! We shall see if your new chief is up to the task," he smirked. In a split of a second he transformed into a growling grey wolf and started walking toward Angelique, jaws opened.

Ma'Dika stepped back, with one hand pushed Angelique forward and said calmly but firmly, "You can take him on."

"Let's see what you are made up of, chief," growled Sam, mocking Angelique.

Following a brief moment of panic, under the watchful eye of Ma'Dika, Angelique recalled her initiation into witchcraft and quickly transformed into Black Panther.

Both walked in a circle sizing up one another. With a raised paw, Angelique harshly propelled Sam in the air as he leapt off to attack her. Landing on his back on the red clay ground Sam quickly recovered by taking the form of a king cobra and hissed his way toward Angelique. In retaliation Angelique transformed into an African honey badger lunging and swiping at Sam with her claws.

In her attempt to pin him and bite him near the head, Sam managed to slither away, giving himself just enough time to switch into a cheetah and resumed his attack.

Fending off Sam's cheetah bites with her sharp honey badger claws and pointed teeth, Angelique found his groin which she grabbed with her teeth, crushing them ferociously. With a weakened Sam struggling to get back on his feet, Angelique moved a few metres away only to come back charging, head down, horn on target as a three-thousand five-hundred kg white rhinoceros.

Having to admit he was facing a more worthy opponent and fearing a fatal injury from the battle, Sam galloped away with his cheetah's legs and disappeared into the bushes.

Angelique stopped in her tracks, breathing heavily. She slowly regained her human form, collapsing on the ground from exhaustion. A proud Ma'Dika danced and chanted tribal songs of victory around Angelique's limp body before piggy-backing her, with supernatural strength, to the hut.

She served a feeble Angelique a traditional herbal infusion and placed her under strict orders to rest that entire morning.

The battle against Sam was her first test as a witch which she passed with flying colours. However, it taught her a valuable lesson; switching shapes uses up a vast amount of energy. As per her custom, Ma'Dika was on hand to share her wisdom by divulging to Angelique once she was back on her feet later in the day that regular self-meditation was the panacea to energy safeguarding.

Chapter 10
Angelique Marries Abaddon

It was about eleven p.m. when Ma'Dika briefed Angelique on the event that awaited them on her last night in the village. The young sorceress was notified that she was to be betrothed to Abaddon the ruler of the underworld.

"This is the greatest honour any witch can receive. You have to consider yourself lucky. Tonight will be a great ceremony and feast in the underworld," said Ma'Dika. There was no-one greater nor more powerful than Abaddon indicated Ma'Dika. With him by her side Angelique was on her way to becoming one of the most powerful human beings on the planet. The old woman painted a glorious and happy future awaiting Angelique as Abaddon's bride.

She also laid to rest once and for all her earlier fears over future amorous relationships by reiterating that her union to Abaddon would by no means interfere with future relationships she may wish to pursue in the physical world. However, the proviso was Angelique would have to seek consent from Abaddon prior to engaging in certain types of relationships out of respect. Finally, she forewarned Angelique that Abaddon would present her with a wedding gift at the ceremony and would demand one from his bride in return.

"Whatever he asks, you must give. No one says no to King Abaddon," cautioned Ma'Dika.

"If it is in my power to give I will, but he has all he can desire, so what type of gift would he be likely to request?" questioned Angelique.

Ma'Dika's answer was snappy and final, "All you need to know is that it will be in your power to give and you must give it!"

On the wedding night they both came out of their bodies by pressing on their tattoos to enter the underworld. A couple of sirens were already in the bride chambers expecting them. The first one was blonde with silky, long straight hair and the second was Asian with sultry wavy dark locks. They were clothed in sheer long dresses which covered their tails. Angelique was surprised they had enough strength in their tails to stand up. They had come with the special assignment to dress Angelique for the wedding ceremony. Her bridal apparel was a gift from Queen Amazonia, her godmother.

The sirens dressed Angelique in a body-hugging gold embroidered high neck mermaid appliqué sheer lace gown. The see-through underlining revealed the curves of Angelique's slender frame, whilst intricate detailing maintained her modesty. A long sheer cape was draped on her shoulders and a golden spiked halo crown, encrusted with withered red roses, was placed on her head. Her black astral afro hair fell all the way down to the floor.

She looked as stunning as the sirens and to her amazement she had their sinister pale green eyes as well, which was a sharp contrast to her natural brown. She was handed a bouquet of shrivelled red, white and yellow roses.

Ma'Dika pulled out all the stops for the occasion as well, by transforming herself into a sexy fourteenth century brunette venetian courtesan.

A driverless black limousine ferried the bridal party to Abaddon's main temple that was located in the Bermuda triangle inside the Atlantic Ocean. The temple was a spectacular domed monument constructed with black marble and gemstones, crowned by a cruciform lantern. Surrounded by four domed chapels in its four corners, it was the tallest and grandest temple in both the physical and the astral world. The name of the temple was 'the glory of Abaddon'. The entire interior of the temple was sumptuously decorated with black and white marble, architectural sculptures and gilding. Mammon welcomed Angelique in the luxurious atrium and escorted her into the main chapel where thousands of guests had come from the four corners of the universe. At the sound of the trumpet, Angelique made her entrance on Mammon's arm. Her legs were shaking and her heart pounded inside her chest. The guests stood from their seats and the orchestra played the underworld wedding march which was a combination of classical and heavy rock music. The walk to the altar was slow and long. Among the guests present, Angelique spotted her dad, Amazonia, her godmother, Sorceress Funke, many famous performers, sports personalities, scientists, politicians, kings, queens, business people, priests, warlocks and witches. The elite of the world including famous and influential individuals – she only heard about in the media until now – and la crème de le crème of the netherworld had all turned up to witness the union of Abbadon to his seventh bride. Angelique was taken by the sheer size of the event and lacked the fortitude of mind to fathom what she was witnessing.

An underworld clergyman, adorned in a scarlet ecclesiastical mantle known as 'cappa magna' and a tall damasked mitre, awaited Angelique at the golden pulpit. He held a book with the inscription 'The hidden mysteries of Babylon'. A few steps back from the pulpit was an imposing eight-foot black marble chair with two marble pillars on either side reaching up to the temple's ceiling. Mammon parted from Angelique at the foot of the altar facing the minister and took a seat at the front row. The music stopped and an announcement was heard on a loudspeaker, "Ladies and gentlemen, now we welcome, under your applause, Abaddon, king of the bottomless pit!" The entire congregation cheered while a black swarm of flies and locusts flew inside the chapel and headed for the marble chair. Upon reaching the seat, the insects assembled together to form an extremely attractive man. He had tanned skin and glowing interminable long black hair that disappeared in the aura of darkness that enveloped him. Abaddon was eight feet tall but for the wedding he took on the height of six feet four which was more befitting to his pairing with Angelique. He was clothed in black from head to toe; he waved at the guests and gave Angelique the most endearing smile as he sat down.

The clergyman took Angelique by the hand and presented her to Abaddon. She bowed at his feet, her eyes fixed on the scarlet flooring.

"Hello, my angel," he hushed softly, lifting up her chin delicately with his finger. The sound of his voice was like the sound of many strings of instruments. His eyes were a whirlwind of hypnotising darkness, a total abyss. Angelique was beguiled by his beautiful appearance. He definitely had the looks, he was perfect. But she also sensed danger emanating from his entire being. For lack of better words, the best way she could describe Abaddon was; the embodiment of darkness.

"Your majesty," she said.

As the clergyman proceeded with the pronouncement of marriage, standing in front of Abaddon, Angelique seriously questioned her actions and involvement with the spirit world. But she knew there was no turning back. That night, in the presence of the universal host, Angelique became the seventh bride of Abaddon, the ruler of the underworld. He slid ten dazzling diamond rings on each of her fingers, placed a cast iron crown encrusted with precious stones on her head and promised to love, protect and provide for her always.

The new bride's wedding gift consisted of trunks filled with jewellery and precious stones, which was delivered by fifty bejeweled white elephants mounted by Indian fakirs.

In return Abaddon requested two wedding gifts from Angelique which the minister read out: the first was her fertility, not to ever bear children. If Angelique was to accept she would every month offer the blood from the first day of her periods to Abaddon as a sacrifice and dedication of her fruitfulness to the lord of the underworld. The second request was the vow of celibacy in the mortal world, which allowed dating but no marriage to any mortal for as long as she lived. Abaddon's request was an extremely high price to pay for good luck and fortune in Angelique's opinion. Marriage and children were topics she had yet to make up her mind about. However, forsaking them altogether seemed rather brutal. Ma'Dika had been a tad economical with the truth concerning the union. This was very much a real matrimonial commitment, the only twist being that infidelity was tolerated, in today's language it would be labelled an 'open marriage'.

Angelique hesitated but dared not disrespect Abaddon in the presence of the guests by refusing him. Moreover, she had gone too far and there was no turning back now. With heaviness in her heart she granted Abaddon his petition.

Their union was sealed with a kiss and legalised with a contract Angelique had to sign with her blood. The clergyman warned her using words she already knew too well, "This contract cannot be broken!"

The wedding banquet was a lavish and sumptuous affair. Held in the deep sea perfectly landscaped gardens, astral creatures mingled freely with humans, savouring the finest cuisine and alcoholic beverages from across the universe. Marcus Lancs and Tisha Lowe, the music industry's most popular recording artists, delighted the guests with their latest hits. Angelique threw some shapes on the dance floor, under the envious glares of Abaddon's other six wives. They each had a special high chair allocated to them where they sat surrounded by an entourage of maids and servants; whilst the new bride took her place beside Abaddon. Had their attendance not been a three whip rule, none of them would have been present. The arrival of a new bride to them signified heightened competition for their husband's attention. So feasting was the last thing the wives in post were in the mood for. Interestingly, contrary to what Angelique would have thought, not all the wives were beautiful. Some happened to be quite plain looking. But they all had one thing in common; they were humans.

Angelique squeezed in a bitter-sweet moment with her father by the garden's water fountain, prior to him being taken back to the underworld slave factory. Richard was only granted a couple of hours to attend his daughter's wedding. He was extremely proud of his daughter. Every sacrifice he had made as far he was concerned was worth it, because he was finally going to exact revenge on his arch-enemy Bjork Janssen. Seeing him at Angelique's wedding made him seethe with rage, but he comforted himself knowing that the engine that was to bring about Bjork's fall from grace had been set in motion from the moment Angelique said 'I do'.

In addition to being introduced to heads of states, prominent entrepreneurs and famous artists, Angelique was presented to the members of Abaddon's council of sages, also known as the princes of Sheol. These seven men worked closely with Abaddon and were the world's most powerful warlocks: Arjun Roshan, Santiago Montoya, Burt Smith, Bjork Janseen, Wu Chan, Chris Adler and Jamal Abdul. Out of all the sages, Bjork Janssen was the one Angelique paid the most attention to. As the reigning Chief Executive of WAXXA Global Bank, the world's largest Investment Bank, it was his job and seat she would step into. All the sages except Bjork were accompanied by their spouses. Jashwanti, Arjun's wife, was absolutely hilarious. They instantly became friends.

The ceremony concluded with a display of fireworks in the underwater skyline. After the guests' departure, Angelique was ushered by the mermaids to Abaddon's private luxurious chambers located inside the temple. She spent some time contemplating the massive bed sprinkled with dry red rose petals, pondering on what was coming next. Could it be that she was about to get intimate with a non-human? Bizarrely that thought had not crossed her mind until now.

Abaddon walked in through the door smiling at Angelique, wearing nothing but a pair of white-lined trousers. He had the perfect torso and his floating hair was never ending. He offered Angelique a flute of champagne to help her unwind. Once again he professed his love for Angelique and cautioned her that he expected nothing less in return from her. His entire presence was hypnotising. As they spoke, he lifted her dress, pinned her against the wall and took her. The lovemaking was raw, long, intensely pleasurable, yet devoid of warmth and emotions. Abaddon was in control throughout their amorous session. Before flying away in a swarm of flies and locusts, he informed Angelique that he planned to visit her often and that they'd have plenty of time to get to know each other better.

In the wake of her marriage, Angelique was crowned chief of the Tumbu's tribe in the presence of her family members, the village elders and the Tumbu's community. Oluchi and the twins specially drove to the village to attend Angelique's coronation. Various members of the Sakola family travelled from different parts of the country to pay their respect to the new chief. Ma'Dika took Angelique around the village accompanied with African drum beats and tribal dancers. At the end of the celebrations, before her departure, village elders and people from the village brought presents to Angelique to honour her as their new chief of tribe. To the majority, the coronation was a tradition people from tumbu merely kept, unbeknown to all and her relatives – aside from Sam and Marie – Angelique was now officially one of the most powerful witches of her time.

ISABELLE KAMALANDWA BRYAN

Chapter 11
Hello Laurent

"Arrghhh baby.. " Angelique moaned and purred like the cat that got the cream, as Laurent gently stroked her back and nibbled her ear lobes. They were both enjoying a Sunday morning lie in. Due to work commitments Angelique's life had grown hectic to such an extent that unscheduled moments of intimacy with Laurent had become extremely rare. This was the first day off Angelique had managed to take in a year since being appointed EMA (Europe, The Middle East and Africa) Vice President at WAXXA Global, a minor post until she fully ascended to the top position. Understandably she was determined to enjoy each second of this golden opportunity, and so was Laurent.

Basking in Laurent's amorous prowess, the chain of events that ensued her father's death fast forwarded in Angelique's mind. Merely a year after her initiation and union to Abaddon, Angelique was offered the post of regional Director at WAXXA Global, which led to a promotion the subsequent year in the shape of her current role. Her life had indeed undergone a dramatic transformation. She had attained a level of wealth she had never been previously exposed to. It was crazy money. She was earning enough to spend many lifetimes over. She flew across the globe in private jets and had enough shoes to fill a department store. Ordinary men could only dream of reaching such heights.

Her primary residence was a two-storey Victorian property in the prestigious Primrose Hill in West London. In addition, she was the proud owner of a luxury apartment in New York and a villa in Antibes in the South of France which Laurent had no knowledge of. She had to exercise maximum discretion not to draw attention to the occult source of her abrupt prosperity. Witches were welcome characters in fiction not in real life.

Her bursting career however aroused Laurent's curiosity who at various occasions queried her rather fast escalation on the career ladder in WAXXA within such a short space of time. Not being at liberty to share her dark secret with the man she shared her life with pained Angelique. Laurent was not only her lover but her best friend and her sounding board. Sadly, openness and honesty in a relationship were no longer a luxury Angelique could afford as a result of her association with the underworld. It was not given to Laurent to comprehend the mysteries of the dark side. Therefore, she endeavoured to be as vague as she possibly could whenever Laurent brought up the topic. Her ready-made answer was that the role came by the recommendation of one of her father's old university friends who owed the latter a favour.

Whilst her new lifestyle was on a high, the spirit side lacked in the fun department. There were strict and challenging demands on a sorceress of her stature and her sexual encounters with Abaddon were far too frequent, depraved and devoid of warmth. Hence, she looked forward to her lovemaking with Laurent.

Notwithstanding, the sense of power she held was exhilarating. Her ability to manipulate people and situations in her favour was hugely invigorating. On top of her day job, as part of her new duties as one the most powerful witches in the world, she had to attend secret meetings in the spirit world, in different earthly continents.

Laurent turned Angelique over and kissed her passionately. During that moment of intimacy, Angelique was able to let go of all the tension and apprehension she had been feeling about her fast approaching challenge campaign for Bjork Janssen's seat as president of WAXXA global.

"Oh Laurent, that was amazing," said Angelique panting with her body still quivering from their coupling.

"You are delicious, my precious Angelique. I can make love to you all day long," whispered Laurent while his hand wandered over her naked body. His hair was long, wavy and shaggy, he looked so hot.

"Really? So what are you waiting for," teased Angelique. She pulled him toward her, and that Sunday they repeatedly made love as the sun rose over Primrose Hill.

Chapter 12
The Proposal

Ecstatic was too weak a word to describe the surge of emotions Laurent was subjected to at the idea of spending a whole Sunday with Angelique. He was conscious that their relationship had been dropping down her priority list, with WAXXA far in the lead. Not only was he beginning to feel neglected, but he was worried the woman he loved was slowly slipping away from him. Moreover, he had noticed Angelique's demeanour was different since her return from Africa. Although he could not quite put his finger on it, he detected there was a new side to Angelique he was unfamiliar with and felt excluded from. He abhorred feeling that way, therefore whenever these thoughts would arise he'd do his best to brush them off and made a concerted effort to convince himself that the change was only part of her mourning process and she would soon snap out of it and return to her old self.

Angelique was the love of his life; he was determined to hold on to her and he believed marriage was the most effective way to achieve his goal. Although she had twice rejected his marriage proposal, under the excuse that she was not ready, he carried his mother's diamond ring everywhere with him awaiting an opportune time he would present it to Angelique, hoping he would strike it lucky a third time.

Furthermore, Laurent was of the opinion that marriage was the natural progression in their relationship, given that they had been together for over five years. Granted Angelique was a lot more successful in her career than he was. His managerial position at the GenoBio Foundation was no match for Angelique's high-flying job at WAXXA Global. Nevertheless, despite their professional gap, Laurent was convinced their love for one another was all that mattered. Besides, only marriage would lay to rest the concerns he had about the increased frailty in their relationship.

At midday they finally managed to crawl out of Angelique's house. Having satisfied the full lust they had for each other's bodies, they went for a stroll around Hampstead village where they picked up some sandwiches and salads from their favourite delicatessen in Primrose Hill and headed to the park for a picnic.

An oak tree by one of the Hampstead ponds provided the perfect shade as Laurent and Angelique put down the blankets on the grass which was covered with daisies. They joyfully ate lunch and drank expensive wine, watched from a distance by the seasonal proud herons. The breeze blew softly whilst swallows chuntered away; Laurent's head gently rested on Angelique's lap as she lovingly ran her fingers through his soft and wavy locks. Without uttering a word, they quietly savoured a moment of perfect intimate silence.

Perceiving it to be the adequate romantic moment, Laurent's ensuing act was to be the catalyst that would forever seal the fate of his love story with Angelique.

Angelique shut her eyes and allowed her thoughts to wander away, oblivious to Laurent's intentions. He slipped his fingers in his jeans pocket and pulled the ring out of his pocket. Holding onto it, he gently kissed her on the lips, got on one knee and spoke the words that would bring Angelique's world crashing down.

"Angelique ma chérie, tu sais que je t'aime. You're the love of my life. If you truly love me as much as I love you, then marry me."

Laurent had never looked so adorable as he waited on one knee for Angelique's response holding out the beautiful white gold single solitaire diamond ring that had been an heirloom in his family for generations.

"Don't turn me down for a third time chérie, I won't be able to bear it," whispered Laurent. He had the imploring eyes of a life prisoner begging for clemency.

Angelique's initial instinct was to propel herself in his arms and shout loudly, yes. In reality, she knew that this could never be because she would be disobeying the commands of the underworld. Agreeing to Laurent's proposal would be no different to her putting a gun on her temple and his for that matter and firing the bullet. No disobedience was tolerated in the underworld and as a consequence was severely punished. She had witnessed the various ways people who disobeyed were chastised and had no desire to find herself in a similar position. A few cases sprung to Angelique's mind; Ella, one of the witches from Canada was beaten up to the point of non recognition by spirits when she attempted to leave the underworld after she fell in love and became pregnant. She lost her unborn child and her lover mysteriously disappeared. Doctors from the underworld attended to her wounds, but six months after her recovery she committed suicide.

Sanjeev Khan, a warlock and Indian magnate, saw his entire multi-million dollar fortune vanish in the space of two months after he challenged the underworld by his refusal to deliver his brother Kabir Khan to Abaddon. Kabir was some type of activist who belonged to an obscure rival group. Through his activities he turned away many men and women from the underworld, therefore increasingly posed a threat to the stability and operating system of the underworld. International newspapers controlled by the underworld launched a smear campaign against Sanjeev accusing him of fraud and embezzlement which resulted in the loss of investors and subsequent bankruptcy. In that same year his model wife left him and took away his two teenage boys who later mysteriously got involved in the consumption of heroin. He suffered a nervous breakdown and was institutionalised in the New Delhi mental hospital where he spent the rest of life.

Finally, Chidi Okafor, a famous Nigerian entertainer, aired his discontentment about the underworld system on the Nigerian national television. He went as far as exposing some of its secrets and confessed he wanted out. Two weeks after his interview Ola had a sudden heart attack and died in his villa in Abuja. His soul was taken to the underworld by the collector spirits where he has been serving as a slave until his given number of years would be fulfilled.

Angelique was conscious that Laurent was probably one of the loveliest men she had met. As a boyfriend she could not fault him, he was perfect. She had no doubt of his love for her. He would definitely make a perfect husband some day, unfortunately not to her, because of the vow she made to Abaddon. Undeniably, she was extremely fond of Laurent and even possibly in love with him, but she would never be the wife he so much desired. It was then it dawned on her that she was witnessing the ultimate moments of her love story with Laurent Chevalier.

Angelique felt tears tingle in the corner of her eyes before they started streaming down on her face, smudging her black mascara.

"Why can't we just keep things as they are?"

Laurent was shocked and deeply hurt Angelique was turning him down again and for the third time he was left in the cold.

"What is it Angelique? Don't you love me?" questioned Laurent.

"You know I love you," said Angelique gently caressing his cheek. "Is marriage at all necessary? These days people do have successful relationships without signing a piece of paper."

"I am not most people!" snapped Laurent, pushing her hand away. "I don't recognise you anymore Angelique. Something has happened to us and I don't like it. The only way I can really be sure we are for real is if you agree to go all the way with me," Laurent defiantly held out the ring to Angelique.

"Laurent don't do this ..." begged a sobbing Angelique.

The pain Laurent felt was indescribable. Angelique had shot an arrow in his heart and left him bleeding. All went silent around them as they looked deeply into each other's teary eyes. Laurent knew it was the end. Theirs was not a happy ending. He finally got up and said, "Goodbye Angelique".

Angelique helplessly watched a heartbroken Laurent walk away from her life on a Sunday afternoon. She was distraught knowing that she had not only lost a great lover but also a dear friend. The underworld truly had its grip on Angelique. She wept bitterly because she knew she would never see Laurent again. Her life was no longer hers.

Chapter 13
Meet the Janssens

'What do you mean that I am not going to be your successor?!' Erika jumped off from the Sloane leather sofa where she was comfortably sitting and stood in front of her father demanding an explanation.

Bjork deliberately chose to break the news to his eldest daughter after their traditional family Sunday dinner, simply because he wanted to eat his favourite meal, the pork roast and potato cakes at peace before the hurricane he foresaw would come his way after he had made the fatal announcement.

He had known for a while that the Janssens' sorcery mantel that had been passed from one generation to another was to end with him. His doom was ratified the day that cursed Angelique Sakola walked down the aisle to marry Abaddon. He would have preferred to take this disturbing news about the sinister fate awaiting his family to the grave. However, in the face of the fait accompli of his imminent downfall, he had a duty to prepare his wife and children for his departure.

Erika furiously paced up and down in the spacious living room in the Janssens' luxurious property located in the affluent Stockholm residential suburb of Ekerö. Everything about Bjork's lifestyle oozed opulence. His motto in life was 'only the best would do'. He lived up to his own expectations. He was the proud owner of a twelve-bedroom manor by Lake Mälaren, just a couple of miles away from the royal family residence. Surrounded by oak trees, the chateau boasted two swimming pools, stables, a one hundred and fifty seat cinema theatre, a private disco, two tennis courts and a fully fitted gym, which included a Jacuzzi and sauna. Bjork inherited the CEO office at WAXXA Bank from his father, Boris, who was a sage in Abaddon's council. A canny businessman, Bjork firmly established himself as the undisputed magnate of the banking industry clinching the coveted title of businessman of an era awarded by Forbes.

He prided himself on his professional achievements as well as being a model father for his daughters. Erika had never wanted for anything in her thirty years of existence – that was until now. Sadly, on this occasion, for the first time in his life, he could not indulge her, matters were out of his hands. No one could fight Abaddon and win.

Bjork attempted to the best of his abilities to calm his daughter down without success. She wanted an explanation and details which Bjork did not feel inclined to provide.

Erika was a typical Swedish beauty of slim figure, 5ft 8in tall, straight shoulder length golden blond hair, tanned skin and big blue eyes. A truly gorgeous girl and chief executive and founder of 'Svart Katt', a Swedish-based clothing brand. The brand had spread across the globe with both Erika and Carla at its helm, and as the faces of 'Svart Katt'. Equally as pretty as Erika and a professional model, Carla, the Janssens' second daughter, was adorned with a different type of beauty: she had wavy long jet black hair, five foot seven inches tall, rosy pale soft skin, with brown eyes. Aside from their physical attributes and business acumen, the Janssen sisters, under their mother's supervision, were the top witches in Western Europe.

Bjork was issued from a long line of Swedish warlocks dating back to the Vikings. Similarly, Greta's lineage was equally deeply rooted in Nordic sorcery. Therefore, her union to Bjork was a merger of two powerful occult clans.

"Calm down Erika," said Greta running her perfectly manicured fingers in her silky straight hair. Over the years she substituted her dull brown hair with a vibrant warm auburn colour. At fifty-six she was still a strikingly handsome woman.

"I understand your disappointment, but nothing will be solved by getting upset," she continued calmly. Greta was a cold and calculative woman convinced that she had perfect knowledge of everything concerning her husband. She did not see this coming. The underworld edict of sorcery clearly stated that membership to the council of sages could only be acquired through birthright to be inherited by the sages' firstborn. In their case Bjork's seat in the counsel of the sages by right belonged to Erika. Greta had great difficulty reconciling what she knew to be an established fact with what had come out of Bjork's mouth. Although she was baffled at the sudden twist of events, it was not in her nature to lose her cool. She slowly turned to Bjork and stared at him with her piercing hazel eyes, "I am sure your father has a perfect explanation."

Bjork deliberately avoided eye contact with his wife. She could always read him as plain as a book. He was a broken man. "This matter was out of my hands, you know fully well Abaddon has the power to change the rules," he muttered.

Erika was in despair mode and Bjork sympathised with her. She had trained and applied herself studiously to the art of sorcery since her youth. She was a fully accomplished witch and deserved taking over from him. Bjork, on the other hand, could not muster the courage to confess to his family how Richard Sakola got the better of him. It enraged Bjork that Richard, who was a much lower ranked sorcerer than him, succeeded in causing his downfall. He regretted not killing him when he had the chance. By letting him live Bjork enabled Richard to join forces with Ma'Dika and achieve what no mortal had previously succeeded in doing; getting a member of Abaddon's council of sages removed from his seat.

Life as Bjork knew it, took a major turn when he was summoned to Abaddon's courtroom the day following his wedding to his seventh bride, Angelique, only to be informed by the ruler of the underworld of a blood grievance against the Janssen clan. Bjork discovered that the claim was lodged twenty-six years ago by Richard Sakola in the name of his daughter Angelique Sakola, the betrothed of Abaddon. The grievance was to take effect on the day of her nuptials.

Seated inside the elevated judge bench, Abaddon was uncompromising. In the underworld courtroom Abaddon was judge, jury and executioner.

"An offence against my bride is an offence against my person," he said.

Bjork sank to his knees from the accused box, "Your lordship, far from me was the intention to offend you."

"Regrettably you have! The blood offence demands retribution," Abaddon stated.

Bjork was livid as Abaddon pronounced the sentence, "Bjork Janssen, I sentence you to death by execution. As retribution Angelique will be assigned both your positions in my council of the sages and as the next CEO of WAXXA."

Bjork sank to the floor and gasped in terror upon hearing Abaddon's sentence.

"Needless to say, this is a battle she won't lose," concluded Abaddon.

In a desperate bid to preserve his family's legacy Bjork leaped up and threw himself at Abaddon's feet and pleaded his cause; "Master please remember my forefathers served you faithfully and never failed you. Don't blot out my clan's name. I beg you to show mercy."

"You ought to know mercy is a word that does not exist in my vocabulary." Abaddon replied sharply. "My decision is final. You are dismissed!"

From that day on, the clock for his doomsday had started ticking.

"So dad, if Erika will not succeed you, who will then?" Carla's soft voice was heard for the first time since the conversation had begun.

Filled with shame and disappointed in himself Bjork struggled to find the words whilst Erika fixed her questioning eyes on him.

Sat quietly in the far corner of the sofa, Greta looked intensely at the flickering flames burning in the fireplace. Her brain was racing a hundred miles an hour. She had been in the underworld game since her birth and she knew her husband was an extremely powerful warlock who served Abaddon with devotion. What could have happened? Suddenly it dawned on her, she knew.

"Richard's daughter..." she murmured, answering Carla's question, her eyes still glued to the flames. She sensed something was off the moment the news spread in the underworld that Angelique Sakola had become Abaddon's seventh wife. This could not have been a coincidence. The past came flashing back as if it was only yesterday.

Chapter 14
Greta's Past

"Don't worry so much, I am sure my parents will absolutely adore you." Greta was doing her very best to calm Richard's nerves as they stood at the entrance of the luxury Waldorf Astoria hotel in Manhattan, New York. It was the eighties, and they were in their mid-twenties. Richard and Greta had been dating for three years after a chance encounter at a coffee shop in New York where they were both university students. It was love at first sight. Richard Sakola was the young dashing son of a Congolese chief and Greta Mortensens was a daughter of a wealthy Swedish magnate. Whilst both were initiated into black magic, Greta was a higher ranked witch due to her father's position in the underworld. Although not a sage, Magnus Mortensens was an extremely powerful and ambitious warlock who was part of Abaddon's inner circle.

Theirs was a relationship rooted in passion. She was intoxicated with his virility and he was mesmerised by her delicate Scandinavian charm.

"I am more concerned about their reaction when you tell them about this," he placed his hand gently on her slightly swollen stomach. Greta was getting ready to make a double jaw-dropping announcement to her parents; first that she was dating a black man and second that she was having a baby with him.

"Don't trouble your pretty afro with this, I will handle my parents. You just need to know that I love you and they'll love you too," she reached up and gave him a quick peck on the lips, took his right hand and led him inside the luxury hotel. Greta was fearless and a free spirit, and those were some of the reasons why Richard was so attracted to the Scandinavian beauty. Frequently frowned upon, interracial relationships required double the amount of work than same race relationships. But Greta stood up to critics and haters by sending a loud and clear message that she couldn't care less about people's perceptions and was determined to live her life however she pleased.

Introducing her African boyfriend to her parents failed to yield Greta's expectations. Despite her almost heroic bravery, family bloodline duties far superseded her romance with Richard, especially since she was her parents' only child. Although the Mortensens were nothing short of courteous and polite towards Richard, behind closed doors both parents were quick to remind Greta that she was destined for greatness but entanglements with Richard would be a stumbling block to her bright future. As for the pregnancy, it was not the big announcement Greta thought it would be, they were alerted of her condition through divination. Expressing their disappointment, they handed her a business card with the contact details of a young man named Bjork Janssen.

"That's the man you are going to marry and together you will decide what to do about your indiscretion," said her father.

"But dad..." disputed Greta, before she was cut short by her mother. "There is no but Greta!" She cupped her daughter's face in her hands, "Just answer my question;

do you want to follow in the footsteps of the Mortensens and be one of a kind in the universe?"

"Yes!" replied Greta without the slightest hint of hesitation.

"Then you need to wake up and see that this young man Richard is not one of a kind like you. He is a no name in the underworld, he is beneath you," her mother said softly.

And that was the end of that conversation. It was settled. A couple of days later Bjork called Greta and they agreed to meet at a small Jewish deli in Manhattan. Over deep filled pastrami bagels and orange juice, Greta learnt that Bjork Janssen was a budding banker and powerful warlock on his way to inherit his father's seat in the Abaddon's council of the sages. Aside from his professional credentials, he was also drop dead gorgeous, with clear deep sea blue eyes and shoulder length blond locks. Greta was instantly attracted to him. Although her feelings for Richard were more intense, the prospect of a life by Bjork's side seemed more up to her standards than one by Richard's. They both had so much in common. She had to think with her head. Moreover, Bjork was extremely convincing. He courted her for a few weeks relentlessly. He was charming and romantic. He pulled out all the stops in his efforts to win her heart.

One night, he took her for a stroll in central park at midnight where they climbed up a large cherry blossom tree from which they astral projected into Abaddon's court. Greta's first meeting with Abaddon was overwhelming. She had been a witch since her birth, but until then never had the privilege to come face to face with the ruler of the underworld. Abaddon spoke kindly to her and guaranteed her a great future as Bjork's spouse. He promised her riches and glory and offered her an impressive black pearl jewellery set containing a necklace with matching earrings, bracelet and ring as a gift.

From then on, Greta's mind was made up, the encounter with Abaddon had sealed the deal. She decided that she'd had her fun with Richard and would be sad to let him go and would greatly miss him – especially the sex which was spectacular – but it was time for her to step into a higher purpose. The evening after her meeting with Bjork, Greta planned a seductive romantic meal for Richard which culminated into a séance of mad crazy sex. It was her way of saying farewell, he did not know it. In the morning she made him breakfast in bed, they kissed goodbye on their way to university and Richard never saw Greta again. She had caught the flight to Stockholm where Bjork accompanied her to a private clinic to abort the pregnancy. Three months later they were wed and she became Mrs Greta Janssen.

Chapter 15
What Greta Didn't Know

It took Richard time to recover from his break-up with Greta. He was left confused by the entire incident. He never saw it coming. At no point did it cross his mind that his feelings for Greta were not reciprocated. She was a cold-hearted woman who broke his heart into pieces. Meeting Oluchi, a year later, during a business trip to Lagos, reignited in Richard deep emotions he thought were long dead and buried. His feelings for Oluchi stirred him to trust in love again. Oluchi was the youngest daughter of a Yoruba 'Igue' which means chief. She was beautiful, fair skinned, and voluptuous with never ending curves. She was not a witch, which greatly pleased Richard. He felt after his terrible experience with Greta he wanted a normal woman. They were soon married after dating for a few months.

Richard loved Oluchi, even though challenges in their fertility journey drove him to take a second wife, Marie. The union with Marie was a mere act of formality to appease his family who were pressuring him for an heir. Oluchi was the love of his life, child or no child wouldn't change that. Richard made sure he constantly re-affirmed his love for Oluchi. Angelique's unexpected arrival was for Richard a sweet miracle, the cherry on the cake.

Richard's joy was complete, the memory of Greta was behind him, or so he believed until Ma'Dika showed up on his doorstep a few weeks following Angelique's birth. The purpose for her visit was to recommend Richard to designate Angelique as future heiress of the Sakola tribe which would position her as Abaddon's future wife. Richard categorically refused. He told her it was out of the question that he would do such a thing. It was an abomination. Tradition demanded that the first-born male should be chief and that position was reserved for Sam, his first son with his second wife. Deep down the idea of his daughter being associated with the underworld displeased him. He wanted her to be pure like his mother.

As Richard stood firm on his decision and Ma'Dika saw there was no way she could make him change his mind she left. However, she did not give up. She came back two weeks later and this time around she had an ace card up her sleeve. In her bid to convince him to agree to see eye to eye with her she made him an offer he had insufficient willpower to turn down. That offer was revenge against Greta.

The story of Richard getting his heart broken by Greta was no secret to Ma'Dika. As a matter of fact, Richard reached out to Ma'Dika shortly following the break-up seeking a way to make Greta pay for the betrayal and the pregnancy termination. Back then Ma'Dika was a low-grade witch-doctor and had no bandwidth to hurt occultist royalties like Greta and Bjork. Because she was determined to convince Richard about naming Angelique future chief of the Sakola tribe, Ma'Dika reached out to Funke who referred her to the underworld legal counsel.They notified her that according to underworld law, only two categories of people could bring a blood claim against a sage: another sage or one of Abaddon's spouses. Therefore should Angelique marry Abaddon she would be within her legal right to take Bjork to

Abaddon's court of law and demand capital punishment for the killing of her sibling, Richard's aborted child.

On hearing Ma'Dika unfold the revenge strategy, Richard's buried anger against Greta and Bjork resurfaced. There was no way he could allow this opportunity to pass him by, not even his love for Oluchi. He was willing to break tradition and designate Angelique as his successor if this would give him the satisfaction to bring down Bjork and Greta. It was a foolproof plan, but Ma'Dika unveiled that there was a caveat.

"What caveat?" enquired Richard.

"Because there are no sages in the Sakola tribe, if you want capital punishment for Bjork you will have to forgo some of your years and dedicate them to Abaddon's service in the underworld."

"What does that mean? Please speak plainly," urged Richard.

"It means when Angelique reaches the age of twenty-six you will die in the physical world and spend your remaining years in the underworld as a slave."

Richard felt a cold chill run down his spine at the thought of a premature death and leaving behind Oluchi and his child. He took a few days to think it through. He was in turmoil, but deep down knew his desire for revenge was stronger than his commitment to Oluchi and his family. The hate inside of him was greater than the love inside of him.

Following that time of reflection Richard met with Ma'Dika again at his house, where he accepted the deal. They shook hands and the wheel was set in motion. Richard kept his decision a secret from Oluchi until moments before his death, when he instructed her to ensure that Angelique would seek Ma'Dika in the wake of his funeral.

Chapter 16
The Execution

The setting for Bjork's final day was a Roman Flavian amphitheatre located in the underworld kingdom. The mystical version of the legendary battle ground for Roman gladiators was jammed packed without an empty seat in sight. Whilst executions were common practices in the underworld, it was not often that a sage and a spouse of Abaddon were centre stage. Such events were extremely rare and therefore did inevitably draw a large crowd. Every warlock, witch and underworld creature was present for the occasion and would not miss it for anything in the world. The crowd was raucous and excited. It felt like the middle of the afternoon and the air was dry and dusty.

Angelique was first into the arena. Under the loud cheers of the crowd she made her way towards the executioner scaffold to take a position by the guillotine which was going to be used for Bjork's execution. Angelique had no experience in operating the guillotine and this was to be her first execution. In preparation she took some classes from the underworld master executioner ahead of the day. Angelique had the option to allow the master executioner to behead Bjork, but she opted for personally undertaking the task to avenge her father. It was also a show of power.

Confident and focused, Angelique looked intrepid and sexy in her Amazon gladiator suit. She selected a light armour in the form of a white and gold bandeau crop top with a white micro mini skirt. The skirt was held by a diamond encrusted golden belt beautifully revealing her diamond pierced navel. Adorned with heavy black eyeliner Cleopatra style, her hair was pulled back in a long plaited ponytail, complemented with a double-sided gold headdress.

Shortly after, Bjork was escorted out of the amphitheatre tunnel into the arena, with his hands tied behind him, by two medieval monks dressed in maroon robes with matching cowl hats covering their face. Bjork paid little attention to the jibes and insults from the multitude. He had resigned to his fate, his dead gaze was without a thought. His long blond locks were shaved and he was made to wear a plain grey robe for this macabre occasion.

From the imperial box Abbadon attended the event in the company of Mammon, Amazonia, various underworld dignitaries and the sages. The sages' wives and family members and close relatives sat in the second tier seating and this included Bjork's family and Richard Sakola, who had been granted special permission to attend the event. Ma'Dika was by his side.

Bjork slowly ascended the stairs to the scaffold where he was made to kneel down and his head was placed face down in the pillory at the bottom of the guillotine frame, directly below the large blade.

As Angelique placed her hand on the large blade made of steel, she scanned the crowd with her eyes and spotted Ma'Dika and Richard seated by her side with his arms folded. The intensity in his eyes was icy and sombre. This was the moment he lived and died for.

Richard and Ma'Dika's presence was also noticed by Bjork, causing his feeling of distress to grow stronger. They were as a pair of scavengers drawn to the stench of a carcass.

Greta was deeply unsettled by the sight of Richard who was only a few seats away from her. She had secretly kept track of his life over the years and silently grieved his death. Little did she know that Richard was still alive in the underworld. A flood of emotions that had laid dormant for over twenty years began surging back to the surface. Her desperate attempts at making eye contact with her past lover were of no avail. She was disgusted at her own badly-timed insensitivity and emotional betrayal of Bjork. This latter was facing his ultimate hours and she could think of nothing else other than to grab Richard's attention, who in return had not deigned to acknowledge her presence.

The crowd had gone dead silent, waiting, thirsty for blood. The atmosphere in the arena was charged and electric so much so that one could hear a delicate buzz of a fly. Angelique shouted 'This is for you dad!' as she vigorously released the gigantic blade. Bjork's head fell on the ground. She picked it up and raised it towards the crowd. Greta and her daughters wailed in agony, Ma'Dika congratulated Richard with a handshake, Abbadon held out his sceptre to Angelique in approval and the crowd went wild.

In the physical world Bjork's death appeared as a heart attack. Angelique Sakola was appointed as the new Chief Executive of WAXXA Global.

ISABELLE KAMALANDWA BRYAN

Chapter 17
Abaddon's Big Plan

Abaddon has just made his big and ambitious announcement and the underworld was in a state of euphoria. This was a pivotal moment since the beginning of time and a game changer. Abaddon had set his eyes on imposing himself as the lord of the universe by taking full control of the physical world.

Until now Abaddon's influence on the physical world had been fragmented and covert. Although a great majority of people in the physical world were under the influence of the underworld, very few were aware of the existence of the underworld. Abaddon had decided that the time had come for this to change and for both the underworld and the physical world to worship him as lord and master. Abaddon was cognisant that this would be a challenge. While he enjoyed undisputed rulership over the underworld, this was not the case for the physical world. He had enemies and would face strong opposition in the physical world. Therefore, his strategy to subdue humanity was to reach and control every single individual in the physical realm. Abaddon believed that he had sufficient resources and influence to set his plan in motion. He had control of most of the physical world, global banking system, healthcare and communications infrastructures. Through these mediums he would get into every household and each individual who lives under the sun.

At his 'Big Plan' announcement conference Abaddon used some illustrations to show how underworld scientists had finally successfully designed and tested a microchip that, if implanted into a human, would enable the underworld to manipulate them at will. Disguised as a personal data file storage, the chip would be Abaddon's intrusion into the inhabitants of the physical world's private space. The chip would have the ability to track movement, manipulate physical health and the psyche and dictate finance including purchasing power. The microchip would transform Abaddon into the main ruler of the physical world.

Angelique was fascinated by Abaddon's world dominion ambition. It was extremely radical and she was excited when Abaddon invited her and two other carefully selected sages, Arun and Santiago back into his meeting chambers to further elaborate on his plan.

Sporting a fourteenth century gothic style, Abaddon's meetings chamber was lavishly decorated with predominantly red furnishings, except for Abaddon's throne chair which was gold encrusted throughout. A Libabe XXX was posted on each side of the chair. The Libabes were the notorious underworld creatures in charge of security and defence in the underworld. Their duty was to enforce the rule of Abaddon's law in the underworld. They came in the shape of the black-green eight feet tall ghostly heavy built creatures that Angelique saw in her dream. They had the face and the dry scaly skin of a lizard. They also sported a row of elongated scales running from the midline of their necks down to their large tails. The Libabe XXX on the other hand were an upgraded version. They had a similar physical appearance to that of humans unlike the original Libabes. However, contrary to humans they had an impressive pair of bat-like wings and their skin was scabrous and lumpy and of a blue-green algae like colour. Their imposing stature, nine feet tall and their mane of dreadlocks were designed to trigger fear and dread. The Libabe XXX were at the exclusive service of Abaddon. They pre-empted threats to the underworld and conducted covert operations as directed by Abaddon.

After settling on his throne, Abaddon invited Angelique and the sages to take a seat. Angelique felt so proud that she was part of this very exclusive group.

Santiago on the other hand was slightly distracted. This was the first time he was in such proximity to Angelique and he was totally mesmerized by her beauty. She had the loveliest neckline and hypnotising eyes. He was trying hard to keep his composure.

"My humble subjects and Angelique my love," started Abaddon as he glanced over at her with a wink. "Your names are about to enter into the history of the underworld!"

Arun, Santiago and Angelique looked at each other with an air of great satisfaction and pride. Although Santiago's look towards Angelique was more of infatuation than that of pride in Abaddon's mission.

With a sharp hand gesture, Abaddon brought up from the ground a VR of the globe which floated and rotated in the middle of the room. Abaddon stood up and made his way towards the floating globe and the sages gathered around him.

"You are probably wondering why we are looking at the globe? That is because the design of the microchip requires specific minerals if they are to function in the human body: diamond, gold and platinum. In total there are seven such deposits in the world that meet the requirements in terms of their size and production capacity. To implement my plan successfully, I need to get my hands on every single deposit of these minerals. I am glad to inform you that the majority are now in my possession except for three major deposits."

Abaddon pointed with his finger to the locations of each of the three missing deposits: "The Kasai diamond deposit in Congo, the Bangalore gold deposit in India and the Choco Platinum deposit in Columbia."

Abaddon clapped his hands and the globe VR vanished and he turned to the sages; "I am sending each one of you on a mission to acquire the land where those deposits are located by any means necessary. Arun you take Bangalore, Santiago you go after Choco and last, but not least, Angelique my love, you bring me Kasai."

Whenever Abaddon issued a command there was no room for questions, just total obedience. They bowed down their heads and in unison replied, "You can count on us Lord Abaddon".

"Failure is not an option," cautioned Abaddon.

Each in turn swore not to fail. As they were exiting the chambers Abaddon recalled Angelique; "My love, you stay and keep me company and you two can leave".

As the door closed behind Arun and Santiago, Abaddon could be heard saying to Angelique "Come over here my kitten, it has been a while..."

Santiago felt a pinch of jealousy. He wished that it was him with Angelique.

Chapter 18
Matchmaking Game

"I'd like the niçoise salad without the anchovies and instead of boiled eggs can I please have feta, thank you." Jashwanti was being fussy with her food as usual. Angelique thought why order a niçoise if it would end up resembling a supermarket salad? Angelique rolled her eyes in exasperation and ordered a steak frites from the handsome waiter.

"He is cute isn't he?" Jashwanti whispered in Angelique's ear whilst the waiter walked away with their orders.

"I didn't notice," pretended Angelique. Yet she did notice his dark hair, svelte figure and sexy smile.

"Yeah right... liar," retorted Jashwanti. "You need a man!"

Angelique was looking forward to spending the afternoon with Jashwanti, it was great catching up with her friend. They immediately bonded at Angelique's wedding and have been friends ever since. Jashwanti was not only a senior partner in a global law firm based in London, but also a very powerful Indian witch. Owing to their busy schedules, they made a pact to meet up at least three times a year for lunch or dinner in order to prevent their friendship from going stale and keeping it fresh.

This lunch was their first in the aftermath of Bjork Janssen's execution. Eight months had passed since Angelique stepped into the highest post in WAXXA and things were not as smooth as she would have hoped. Her success roused jealousy in many and on her way to the top she had gained powerful lifelong enemies in the shape of Greta, Erika and Carla Janssen. The Janssen women swore to avenge the death of Bjork and Angelique was conscious of it. So spending time with a friendly face and an ally was exactly what Angelique needed.

Lunch with Jashwanti was booked at a highly exclusive bar restaurant in London. It was the later end of spring. Angelique sported long curly brown extensions with blond highlights and selected a simple see-through peach blouse with a pair of light blue jeans and black boots. Jashwanti opted for a traditional round neck short sleeve black day dress which accentuated her latest hair bob with black sandals.

"Leave my love life alone," snapped Angelique. "Talking of love lives, I thought your hubby was joining us today."

"Talk of the devil... here he is," Jashwanti waved at Arjun who was making his way to their table.

Angelique envied Jashwanti to some extent. She was one of those witches married to another warlock. This was the perfect scenario as it somewhat simplified the relationship. They seemed really happy and had two lovely young boys. However, Angelique had nothing to complain about in her own life. Her relationship with Abaddon gave her status that only a handful of witches could achieve in a whole lifetime. Besides, if one day she felt her maternal instincts kick in, there were options available thanks to science these modern days through which she could have children. A consolation prize, although meagre, to compensate for the sad reality that she could not have her own biological babies.

Arjun Roshan was a famous Bollywood producer and, of course, a much-respected and feared Indian warlock. He was polished, more charismatic than good looking and about five foot eleven inches. An utterly heartless sorcerer, he had reached the seventh level in mystical black and white magic and was often used by Abaddon to punish and eliminate those rebelling against the underworld. He was a lethal man to have as an enemy and indeed one to be reckoned with. Luckily for Angelique they got on like a house on fire. She considered this couple as her best friends.

Arjun gave his wife a peck and Angelique a kiss on the cheek before sitting down on the light brown couch by his wife's side.

"Lovely to see you, Arjun. And your hair is shorter," noticed Angelique, "I approve." Arjun had his shoulder length curly hair cut and gelled back.

"Nice seeing you too Angel. I look more grown up with my hair short," quipped Arjun.

Jashwanti caressed the back of Arjun's head, "I think you look sexy and suave my love."

"You are my biggest fan babe," he gave her his seductive smile. After ordering the lemon chicken tagliatelle and a glass of white wine he turned back to Angelique, "So I believe congratulations are in order. How does it feel being the top dog at WAXXA?"

"I can't complain, share prices in most banks have sky-rocketed which is only good news for WAXXA. We could not be in a better position. I am more excited about Abaddon's great plan."

"It is going to be a revolution! I should bring Bangalore home in the next few weeks," bragged Arjun.

"Impressive!" marvelled Angelique. "Abaddon will be pleased."

"I don't mess about, how about you, any progress?" he pried whilst helping himself to a glass of water from the table.

"Yes I am on track. I have information about the company that owns the land in Kasai. It's a mining company called Ndeko Corporation. As I understand it, it's a family business, so I have instructed our lawyers to make them an offer they would find hard to refuse. I don't foresee any hiccups. No one turns down the kind of money I am putting on the table," Angelique replied confidently.

"Excellent," applauded Arjun, "It appears Abaddon chose the right people for this mission. He will know how to reward success as well as failure."

Angelique was pondering on Arjun's statement when Jashwanti cut in, "Enough with all this business talk! Although I too am excited about Abaddon's great plan, this is a fun time, let's eat and talk about more fluffy stuff."

"Such as ...?" Angelique quizzed tucking into her French fries smothered in mayonnaise.

"Like the fact that you have been alone too long."

"May I remind you that Abaddon keeps me fulfilled? Thank you very much."

Jashwanti leaned toward Angelique and put her hand on hers, "You know it's not the same hun."

Although there was room for improvement in the affection department, Abaddon was an accomplished lover. He made Angelique explore areas of sexual intercourse she never knew existed. Nevertheless, Jashwanti was right, sex with a spirit was surreal and empty. Their encounters always left her gratified sexually and vacuous emotionally. It was clear that the missing elements were flesh and blood, warmth and feelings, which spirits are just not gifted with.

"Okay, okay you have a point, but I am busy and have no time to meet people," conceded Angelique.

"Honey, tell her about Santiago," said Jashwanti as she elbowed Arjun.

"What about him?" Arjun seemed confused.

Jashwanti rolled her eyes and lifted her hands in the air, "Men! Remember you said he thought Angelique was very attractive? And he is single!"

"Oh yeah, he could not keep his eyes off you at the meeting with Abaddon, he thinks you are stunning," Arjun gave Angelique a massive grin.

"Hold on a second... Santiago Montaya the sage?" asked Angelique with a hint of curiosity.

"The one and only!" confirmed Arjun with a wink.

Wow! Santiago Montoya! In addition to being a highly ranked warlock, member of Abaddon council of the sages, he was a powerful drug lord who controlled all drug cartels globally. Born in Cali, Colombia, he quickly ascended to the highest echelons of drug trafficking leading him to control — with the backing of the underworld — the distribution of cocaine worldwide. He was el jefe de jefes — or in English the boss of bosses. She was accustomed to seeing him in different meetings, gatherings and most recently when they were summoned in Abaddon's quarters but little did she imagine he fancied her. Santiago was six foot one inch tall, dark shoulder length wavy hair, deep brown eyes, lean and bursting with masses of Latino charm, which Angelique was definitely not insensitive to.

"So, what do you say? Shall we give him your number?" probed Jashwanti with a cheeky smile.

Angelique paused for thirty seconds before replying coyly "why not?".

Chapter 19
Greta's Obsession

Greta fought hard to get Richard's image out of her head but failed miserably at every attempt. After seeing him again in the coliseum she was restless until she gave in to the impulse to seek his whereabouts. To that end, she conjured her trusted divination spirits who indicated he was a slave in the Metropolis of the underworld.

She selected the day of her trip to the Metropolis with much care. Cautious not to arouse Erika and Carla suspicions. She waited until both girls were at the New York fashion week to travel to the underworld capital city.

A taxi driver who embodied a cross between a man and a lizard collected Greta at the Metropolis gateway – the landing terminal for all witches and wizards travelling from earth – and dropped her off at the 'Transit Slave Factory' (TSF), as directed by the divination spirits.

Slaves at the TSF were not allowed external visitors. They were the private property of Abaddon and no one was allowed to visit without the ruler's permission. Greta was fully aware of that rule, so she came bearing gifts for the chief guard and planned to make him an offer he could not refuse. She offered him an immaculate wrapped gift box filled with scurrying white mice in exchange for a visit session with Richard. It was widely known that the rodents were a sought-after delicacy for the inhabitants of the underworld. White mice, specifically, were the only non-human living organisms that could withstand the transition from the earthly realm to the underworld without dying in the process and that bore great significance because once in the underworld they could be juiced for their fresh blood which boasted stimulant properties. Greta's little gift was unreservedly welcome and her request granted.

She was led through a dark corridor to a small square room, which had only two chairs and a table. She sat herself down, and nervously waited. Richard was brought in minutes later. For the first few seconds he was shocked to see Greta and shortly afterwards he was briefly undecided about whether he was pleased to see her or not.

"Hi Richard," Greta greeted him, "Please take a seat." She indicated the empty chair opposite her.

Reluctantly, Richard took the place facing Greta. He could not help but notice what a beautiful woman she still was. The years had definitely been very kind to her.

"Why have you come here?" he interrogated harshly

Seeing Richard brought back to the surface feelings Greta had kept buried for over thirty years.

"I don't know," she murmured.

"That's a first, I have never known you to be uncertain about anything. Why are you here?" shouted Richard banging his fist on the table. "Have you come to laugh at my predicament?"

"You are wrong Richard, if there is someone laughing, it's you. You finally got your revenge. I am miserable."

"Oh really? Good, I am glad you are in pain and

miserable. But that does not answer my question, why are you here?"

"Your daughter killed my husband."

"You and your husband killed my child. We are even."

"I underestimated you, Richard. I did love you though," she confessed.

There was no denying he was still very much attracted to her. He had to keep his cool because Greta was a very calculating and dangerous woman.

"Just go away Greta, this is a farce."

Greta stood up, like a feline in her mating season she seductively strutted toward Richard, "Can I at least get a goodbye kiss?"

She drew her lips close to Richard's, slightly parting them so he could feel the warmth of her aroused breath. Succumbing to temptation, Richard pressed his mouth on Greta's moist lips in a passionate embrace. Tongues, intertwined, they sank into an intoxicating French kiss as their bodies naturally drew towards one another like magnets. For a moment the present had ceased to exist, they were back in Manhattan in the Eighties. They were free to love and be loved, without a care in the world. He wanted her like mad there on that table, on the floor, against the wall, wherever it may be, he wanted her. As he spread Greta on the table, Oluchi's face whizzed before his eyes causing him to stop abruptly. Grabbing Greta by the shoulders he violently pushed her away.

"Go away Greta!" shouted Richard.

Stunned at Richard's sudden back-pedalling and still panting, Greta slowly licked her lips savouring the taste of that moment of savage passion while imagining what could have happened, with her body still shivering with a lingering and an almost gratified sexual yearning.

"Maybe I should have let Bjork kill you," she taunted.

"Maybe you should have," he replied, while he struggled to regain control of his senses.

"Just to warn you now, I will be going after your daughter," threatened Greta as she got off the table and made her way toward the door.

"You are no match for her," retaliated Richard defiantly.

With a hand on the handle, Greta pushed her head back and gave Richard her signature coldest grin and said, "Even the mighty fall". Turning her back on him she slowly shut the door behind her.

Chapter 20
Rachel's Dream

The sound of the Africa cuckoos and swift birds coupled with the gentle swishing noise caused by the swaying of palm tree leaves always gave Rachel a sentiment of peace. She was in her favourite place. Sitting on the Kasai river bank with her feet gently caressed by the warm water. The late afternoon breeze was softly blowing on her auburn locks, stroking her rosy cheeks. This beautiful place was her late husband's dream come true. Rachel Parker met Yves Ndeko when they were both students at Chicago University. They married three years following graduation. Rachel then left her birth country, the United States and moved with her Congolese husband to Congo where they settled in the Kasai region. Yves's family came from a long line of precious metals miners who over time made an immense fortune trading in precious metals. Ndeko Corporation was one of the largest mining companies in Africa and owned around one million acres of land in the Kasai region. After taking the reins of the family mining business, Yves established the 'Ndeko Foundation' to instigate economic growth in the community by encouraging enterprise and providing charitable support to the destitute and marginalised including children, vulnerable women and those with various disabilities. Thanks to Ndeko foundation community investment, Kaisai became the most prosperous region in the whole of Congo.

Rachel had lived the happiest moments of her life with Yves in Kasai. This is where their two beautiful bi-racial children, David and Jessica were conceived. Sadly, on the eve of Jessica's tenth birthday, Yves was assassinated. During a trip to one of the mines, his vehicle was intercepted by an armed group and Yves was killed with two bullets in the head. Yves's assassination had remained a mystery and the perpetrators were never caught. One thing that was clear in everyone's mind is that it was politically motivated, because that year Yves had announced his bid for the presidency of Congo. Yves' untimely death left Rachel at the helm of the Ndeko enterprise.

The Ndeko Foundation children's home was built on a beautiful piece of land overlooking the clear water of the Sankuru river, the main tributary of the Kasai River. The site was Rachel's favourite place whenever she was in Kasai. The scenery was like nothing she had ever seen in the US or in any other part of the world. The native variety of trees and plants were lush and green. The richness of the soil was reflected through its sandy and clay colour. Rachel made a habit of sitting by the river bank, where they could faintly hear the children of the foundation play and laugh in the background. Every now and then the forest giraffe known as the Okapi would show up for a drink on the other side of the river. The Okapi looked like a cross between a deer and a zebra. A visit from this extremely shy mammal, only native to Congo, was a sight to behold and not a common occurrence. Rachel was in luck today. She spotted the movement in the bush that usually announced the arrival of her friend the Okapi. Head first the Okapi emerged from the bush and headed towards the river where it leaned forward for some water. With her face cupped in both hands Rachel observed this endearing creature with admiration. However, today did not feel like a normal day, there was a peculiar aura in the air. With no apparent reason the Okapi became distressed. It looked toward Rachel and began making crying noises. Standing on her feet Rachel tried to make sense of what was bothering the animal. The Okapi's distress call grew louder, Rachel decided that she would cross the river to make her way to the Okapi. As she took the first step she realised the ground was moving from under her like quicksand. It felt like a muddy slippery landslide. She could not move, she was stuck. Suddenly, the clouds darkened and big lumps of sulphur like rain started falling from the sky. In front of her eyes, the rain melted the Okapi to death. Behind her she could hear the cries of the children of the foundation. She looked on and it was chaos. Children were running, screaming and crying. Then she saw an enumerable number of adults, all residents of Kasai, dressed in black rags weeping and looking helpless. They all started to melt and everything around Rachel was melting, even the trees, the sun, and the moon. It was like when water is poured on a canvas painting, washing off the colour and leaving behind a lumpy and bumpy smudge. Tears started to fall from Rachel's eyes, she was witnessing the destruction and carnage of this beautiful land she had grown to love so much. Through her tears she saw a group of men dressed in black uniforms with machine guns walking in the midst of the carnage, laughing. Their boss was a young woman who appeared pleased with the destruction. Filled with rage Rachel grabbed a gun which happened to be by her side, pointed at the woman boss and shouted, "Hey, what have you done to my people! You murderers."

The woman turned towards Rachel and in a swift leap she was standing face to face with her. Although she was up close, Rachel could not discern the face of the woman, it was blurred.

"It's all your fault, Rachel. You could have stopped it!" said the woman in an angry and very distinctive voice.

"I will kill you!" screamed Rachel. She pointed the gun at the woman. She was about to pull the trigger when her eyes were drawn to the woman's chest, she had a massive open wound, a hand that looked like the hand of a beast was crushing her heart. The woman was a heartbeat from death. As Rachel struggled to rationally comprehend what she was seeing, there was a sudden loud sharp sound ringing in her ear. It was her alarm o'clock. She reached out to the bedside table to stop it from ringing. She was in her bed at home in Chicago. It was a dream after all. Albeit, a very strange dream.

Rachel jumped off her bed, she was running late for the Ndeko Corporation virtual board meeting.

Chapter 21
Rachel Won't Budge

Rachel was stunned at how generous the business offer was, the more the presentation went on. Antoine Ndeko, Yves's younger brother and one of the shareholders in the Ndeko Corporation was presenting the takeover bid that just landed from WAXXA corporation. Antoine had called the virtual board meeting to review and vote on this unexpected proposal from WAXXA. Rachel had knowledge of the existence of WAXXA, very often referred to as 'the bank of banks'. Due to their secretive nature, there was very little information about them on the public domain. Unlike the mainstream banks, they had no known headquarters or physical presence. Yet they controlled most of the banking capital in the world. The CEO was a certain Angelique Sakola, a well renowned, astute businesswoman. That is all Rachel knew.

Eight years had passed since Yves's unsolved assassination. Rachel was left as the major shareholder in the company with sixty per cent of shares. The sixty per cent shares included twenty per cent for each of their two children which were under the guardianship of Rachel until they turned twenty-one. The remaining forty per cent were equally split between Yves's cousins Antoine and Jeanne. Yves was an only child and sole and direct heir because Ndeko Corporation was established by his father. However, Yves always held that the business was a family asset and therefore brought in his cousins born from his father's brother.

As she flicked through the bid's documents Rachel increasingly warmed to the idea. Both Antoine and Jeanne had already made it clear that they were in favour of the bid. Hence, the objective of the board meeting was to reach a consensus. Selling might not be such a bad idea after all, reasoned Rachel. Congo had always been unstable politically and plagued by ongoing conflicts. There had been a rise in the number of civil wars, local feuds and cross-border conflicts fighting for control of territory, especially in the mineral rich areas like Kasai. Rachel did not want what happened to Yves to happen to one of her children. The danger of the mine trade permanently lingered at the back of her mind. This was the first time such a takeover bid was received for the Ndeko Corporation and Rachel was inclined to believe that this could be a way out and an opportunity for a fresh start.

However, Rachel had one concern and that was about the Ndeko Foundation. So many children and vulnerable families were supported through the foundation and she wanted somehow to preserve that social side of the business to protect Yves's legacy and keep his memory alive in the region.

"So shall we proceed to the vote?" asked Antoine

"I am in favour of this offer from WAXXA," expressed Jeanne. She had zero business acumen. It was very likely that she would waste all her money on designer bags and shoes. That slightly worried Rachel, but she was also cognisant that at thirty-nine years old Jeanne was a grown woman capable of making her own decisions.

"Thank you Jeanne," responded Antoine. "I am also in

favour of accepting the takeover bid from WAXXA," he asserted. He secretly resented having a foreigner and a woman at the helm of the family business. He had harboured hope that Yves would name him as the guardian for his children's shares, but that did not materialise. Antoine had a well-rounded knowledge of the mining sector. Although it bewildered him why WAXXA made an offer that was thirty per cent above the value of Ndeko Corporation, he was pleased. Getting his hands on such lucrative capital through the sale of his shares would allow him to set up his own mining company and finally land the position he truly deserved.

Turning to Rachel he asked, "What about you Rachel?"

After gathering her thoughts Rachel responded, "I am in favour in principle. However before fully agreeing to proceed I'd need to speak to Angelique to discuss the future of Ndeko Foundation. Ideally, I'd like us to hold on to the Foundation in memory of Yves."

Antoine couldn't care less about the foundation, but for the sake of the deal going smoothly he said, "That's a perfectly reasonable request Rachel. Angelique is aware that we are meeting today and her assistant informed me she would be available to jump in if we needed to speak to her. So I will invite her to join the call."

Antoine entered Angelique's details for the video conferencing. It rang for a few seconds and Angelique appeared on the screen.

"Hello Angelique, nice of you to join us," greeted Antoine.

"Hello, thank you for having me. I am grateful to be here," said Angelique with a smile. Rachel thought Angelique was very classy with her hair pulled back and her black blazer and quite young. Interestingly, Rachel felt a certain familiarity about her.

With the initial introductions out of the way, Rachel shared with Angelique her desire to retain Ndeko Foundation to which Angelique replied: "I totally understand that you would want to preserve your husband's legacy Rachel. And WAXXA has no issue with that whatsoever. We are happy to leave the Foundation out of the deal. However, we would have to relocate its premises. As a sign of our respect to the memory of your late husband we would be willing to acquire new facilities of your choice in the region for your foundation. On top of that we would make a generation donation to your foundation of course."

From that answer Rachel discerned that WAXXA was after the land. The generosity displayed by Angelique was quite over the top, it screamed almost desperate she thought. But all of that did not bother Rachel. What nagged her was the sense of familiarity or déjà vu she felt when Angelique said her name. There was something about her voice and the way she said her name. It was identical to the woman she saw in her dream the previous night. Rachel grew uneasy in the course of the conversation. Her mind was racing. Was this a coincidence or a sign? At the end of the meeting they thanked Angelique for joining the video call and informed her that they would get back to her with a decision at the earliest.

In the wake of the board meeting, Rachel announced, at Antoine and Jeanne's dismay, that she would not vote in favour of the takeover. She did not offer them an explanation for her final decision, but deep down she was convinced that her dream was somehow linked to WAXXA's takeover bid and she needed time and space to process and meditate on the issue. Without Rachel's vote, the deal had stalled.

Antoine wrongly assumed that Rachel's refusal was linked to the location of Ndeko Foundation, so he encouraged WAXXA to amend their offer and agree to maintain the Foundation on the grounds of Ndeko corporation. Still, Rachel did not budge.

ISABELLE KAMALANDWA BRYAN

Chapter 22
Plan B

Angelique was pacing around in her luxurious hotel room in Barcelona. She landed in the city of Gaudi the night before, where she was due to give some keynote speeches at a global investment forum. She had been unable to sleep a wink since receiving the rejection email from Ndeko corporation. The takeover had reached a stalemate and that was a major problem. She needed to think of a plan B, and maybe a plan C. She would go all the way to a plan Z if necessary, failure was not an option. She had to get her hands on those mines, otherwise she would fail Abaddon and that would be catastrophic for her and for Abaddon's great plan. As far as she knew both Antoine and Jeanne were in favour of selling, so her stumbling block was Rachel. The offer WAXXA made was so ridiculously generous that it was pretty clear to Angelique that money could not have been the main driver behind Rachel's decision. She was left with no choice but to resort to coercive methods to guarantee a positive outcome in favour of WAXXA. She needed a plan and really fast.

Angelique had a couple of hours before the start of the conference, so she summoned Jen Wu, her Chief of Staff to her hotel suite to explore alternative strategies to pressurise Rachel to change her mind about selling.

Jen was an extremely intelligent American girl of Chinese descent and a powerful witch who graduated from Harvard Business School. She had been working with

Angelique for the past couple of years. Angelique would not trust her as far as she could spit. Besides, trust was a luxury a woman in her position could not afford. She was the envy of far too many witches and wizards, including Jen, who would backstab her without batting an eyelid if given half a chance to step into her shoes. Nevertheless, Jen's drive and zeal were a great asset to Angelique.

Jen was right on time. She was immaculate as usual in her black trouser suit, Gucci rectangular glasses and hair tied back. Jen did everything to perfection and precision, she performed like a relentless machine which would make the most hardworking person in the world look lazy. Still in her dressing gown, Angelique invited Jen into her suite and led her to a little office inside her hotel suite. Jen had brought Angelique her favourite hot drink, a skinny cappuccino and for herself, an americano.

Whilst sipping their respective beverages, Jen pulled out from her laptop PowerPoint slides containing some intelligence she had gathered on Rachel Parker that Angelique had requested. She began presenting to Angelique; "Rachel Ndkeko Parker is the widow of Yves Ndeko, who was the owner of Ndeko Corporation. Together they had two children. Rachel has dual American and Congolese nationality. The reason why she was able to block the deal is because she controls sixty per cent of the shares of the corporation allocated to her and her children."

"Can we convince the children to sell?" interrupted Angelique.

"No, we can't. Rachel has guardianship until they turn twenty-one and the oldest is eighteen."

'Crap!' swore Angelique.

Jen cleared her throat, slightly amused by Angelique reaction and continued, "My research shows that she has done a stellar job at the head of Ndeko Corporation and has earned a lot of respect in the region and in the mining sector. She is particularly very fond of the foundation. She splits her time between Chicago where she currently resides and Kasai to oversee the business and the foundation. However, the reason she is refusing to sell is not quite clear. At the moment my first hypothesis is that she is refusing to sell to preserve the memory and legacy of her husband. There are reports that her husband was assassinated when he tried to build a political career. So it would make perfect sense she would want to hang on to the foundation."

"Yeah, you could be right, but I did go back and agreed she could keep the foundation on Ndeko corporation premises, but she still turned us down," reflected Angelique. She was convinced there was something else.

"Is she one of us?" asked Angelique. Because they met virtually Angelique could not see whether Rachel had the underworld invisible tattoo on her wrist. If she was a witch maybe she could be convinced differently.

"Well, that's the interesting part," replied Jen with a certain excitement in her voice, "She has no association with the underworld whatsoever. She is not a witch. However, she belongs to a rival group called the fishers."

Angelique was puzzled, "I have never heard of this group, who are they?"

Jen disclosed to Angelique that the fishers were the arch

enemies of the underworld. Their master was a dead god who is alive.

"Dead and alive, that's confusing," uttered Angelique.

"Intriguing, I know," responded Jen.

"How come I have never heard of these fishers?" questioned Angelique.

"You and me both boss. This stuff is news to me too. There is no information about the fishers in the underworld and the reason why we've come to know this is because I had Rachel followed."

"What else did you find out? Do they have powers like us?"

"To be honest my sources could not verify that, but they have uncovered that the fishers have a habit of recruiting members from the underworld to join their camp."

Angelique was having difficulty in digesting the information provided by Jen. Firstly, she had no idea that Abaddon had rivals called the fishers, she always thought that he was the uncontested lord of all. Secondly, she was disturbed that no leader in the underworld including Abaddon had ever mentioned this rival entity. Thirdly, the lack of clarity about what she was contending with was making her very uneasy.

Taking another sip of her cappuccino Angelique interrogated Jen; "So what is your second hypothesis?"

"My second hypothesis is that she knows that the underworld is behind the offer and that's why she refuses to budge," asserted Jen.

Angelique believed Jen was probably right. Although Angelique was not quite sure yet about what type of adversary Rachel was, she was still the enemy. They would need to be more aggressive with her.

Reflecting for a few minutes Angelique said, "We have to keep digging about the fishers. In the meantime, we need something to push Rachel to sell Ndeko mines. What else have you got for me?"

"Well, my research on Congo revealed that the Kasai region is plagued with civil unrest and in that part of the world it's very common for armed groups to take over mines to fund their movements. We could force our way into Rachel's mines through a militia," suggested Jen.

"Actually that's an excellent idea. I know exactly the person for this mission. I have contact with the FFR militia group in Kasai. I will email to you the contact details of their leader who is also a member of the underworld. Get in touch with him and give him whatever he needs to mount a militia take-over of Ndeko mines," ordered Angelique.

"I am right on it," replied Jen quickly getting up onto her feet.

Smart cookie that Jen thought Angelique.

"I want this done ASAP. Just one thing – make sure there is a Libabe present during the operation in case additional support of the other kind is needed."

"No problem, it will be done," nodded Jen while packing up her laptop.

Angelique drew the reunion to an end and Jen left.

Angelique was exhausted, but completely satisfied with the outcome of the meeting with Jen and trusted all would go according to plan. After a hot shower, a power-dressed Angelique was on her way to the conference. She was reviewing her speech notes sitting at the back of her chauffeur driven car, when about five minutes into her ride, the vibration of her smart phone went off, frantically signalling receipt of a text message. Rattling through her deep tote designer handbag, she finally succeeded in pulling the device out. The text message read; "Hola mi reina, a little bird told me you were in Barcelona. Hungry? Santiago M."

Chapter 23
Hello Santi Baby

'Poof like magic...' Angelique's fatigue had vanished following the text message from Santiago Montoya. Straight after the conference she rushed to the beautician for a quick manicure, a facial and to get her eyelashes done. Santiago was due to pick her up from her hotel room at seven p.m. and take her out for a traditional Spanish meal to an undisclosed restaurant. Angelique was not big on surprises, but in this instance she found the element of surprise quite endearing. She did not care where she went for dinner as long as it was with Santiago. He was the best-looking Sage in Angelique's books in addition to being a commanding warlock. She was certain, wherever they went, she'd have a great time. Besides, Barcelona was pretty much Santiago's second home after Colombia, he knew all the best spots.

As time drew closer to seven p.m. Angelique applied the finishing touch to her make-up. The secret was to look as natural as possible without compromising on the quantity of make-up needed. She opted for a rose volupté lip gloss, loose flowing deep brown long curls, purple mini dress, floral scarf, five-inch nude stilettos and she was set to go.

When she opened the door of her hotel room after the doorbell rang at exactly seven p.m. there stood Santiago with a bunch of red roses and his sexy smile. At first glance, he looked stone-cut, six foot one inch, in a white V-neck sweater and blue jeans with freshly gelled hair and an ivory-smooth shave. She greeted him with two kisses on the cheek which was enough time for her to catch a whiff of his cool and masculine perfume. He smelt divine.

Santiago complimented Angelique on looking exquisite as they stepped out of the hotel compound. Secretly, he thanked his lucky stars she had agreed to go out with him. He was lost in admiration the first time he saw Angelique walk down the aisle to marry Abaddon. She was just his type, she was perfect. Although he had dated women of various colour, he had a personal penchant for dark-skinned women. His first love was an afro-Colombian girl he had met while his family briefly lived in the city of Bogota when he was eighteen years old. Ever since, he had developed a soft spot for Nubian women and Angelique was the most fascinating one he had come across. As brave a man as he was, however, he would have never mustered enough courage to ask her out had Arjun not been on matchmaking duties.

They ate at a cosy Argentinean restaurant in the nearby city of Vilanova i la Geltrú, which was a forty-minute drive from Barcelona. Located in a non-touristic part of the coastal town, the family run restaurant specialised in barbecued meats and fresh fish, otherwise known as 'Asodo'. Well known by the locals Santiago was also friends with Pépé the owner who made sure he and Angelique were well looked after and even threw in free drinks on the house. The food was non-assuming, homely and absolutely delicious. Angelique sampled Argentinean cuisine including chimichurris, empanadas as well as the treasured dulce de leche dessert.

The night was warm with the soft sea breeze blowing in

the air. The conversation between Santiago and Angelique flowed effortlessly as they lingered in the restaurant over a glass of wine enjoying the performance of a guitar soloist playing Argentinian folk music. The chemistry between them became more apparent as the evening progressed. Not only were they attracted to one another, but they shared commonality by both being part of the underworld. There was no need for pretending, they were two creatures of the night, a sorcerer and sorceress, getting to know one another, mindful of the peculiar and the abnormal that formed their lives.

Santiago was playful with Angelique. He discovered she was fun and quite bubbly. Before the night was over, he dragged her to the dance floor for a round of slow, sexy salsa. Holding onto Santiago whilst their bodies swayed to the rhythm of the Latino melody, Angelique recalled how good it felt to be in the arms of a real man again and how much she had missed it.

It was around one a.m. when Santiago finally took Angelique back and walked her to the hotel room.

"Thanks, I had a lovely evening, me diverti mucho," Angelique was leaning backward against the wall by her hotel room door, smiling coyly at Santiago, while playing with her hair. She felt like a teenager at the end of a date utterly gagging for that first kiss.

"I enjoyed your company. We should do this again," said Santiago.

"I'd vote for that," she replied.

Santiago moved forward and gave her a kiss on the cheek. "You are gorgeous," he whispered in her ear.

"So are you," she whispered back in his ear.

Santiago paused and gazed into her inviting eyes. The moment felt right for a passionate lovers' kiss. Santiago got a taste of her full African lips as they made out in the hallway like a pair of adolescents. He had to fight the urge to carry her inside, explore every inch of her curvy body and indulge in a night of reckless passion.

Sadly, she was the wife of Abaddon, there were rules to follow. A warlock desiring to be sexually intimate with any one of Abaddon's wives had to seek permission first from the ruler of the underworld otherwise they would be breaking the law. This offence carried the death sentence. Santiago painfully pulled away from his embrace with Angelique and bid her goodnight. Likewise, Angelique was aware of the restrictions imposed on them by the underworld, therefore settled for their brief smooch, but, oh boy, was he a good kisser.

Angelique extended her stay in Barcelona by a few days and saw Santiago every night. He wined and dined her and took her dancing to the trendiest salsa clubs in Barcelona. They carried on seeing each other when Angelique returned to London. The attraction they felt for one another grew to such an extent it became unbearable to hold back. Whenever they found themselves together, it was only a matter of hours before they started snogging like new lovers in heat. It was no different when one evening Angelique invited Santiago back to her house for a nightcap after a party they both attended in central London.

"I can't keep my hands off you," groaned Santiago as he nibbled on Angelique's lips and teased her neck with his tongue.

"Me neither," murmured Angelique caressing the back of his glossy silky short hair.

Stopping in his tracks Santiago sat back on the sofa where they had been making out for the past half hour in Angelique's living room and looked intensely at Angelique and said: "How about we take this to the next level...err, I mean speak to Abaddon?"

Santiago had thought long and hard about his budding romance with Angelique and concluded he wanted her. He was sure of his feelings and was not afraid to approach Abaddon.

Angelique was secretly hoping Santiago would propose moving matters to the next level, but did not want to appear to force his hand into doing it. Aspiring to secure an amorous relationship with Abaddon's wife was not a straightforward process. Abaddon imposed harsh conditions, bordering on unrealistic, to any warlock seeking to mate with one of his spouses. It was known as the 'Abaddon's dowry'. The demands were known to be so outrageous that only the extremely powerful warlocks could meet them while others found themselves forced to withdraw their petitions. The attraction for Angelique in taking her romance with Santiago to the next level was that once Abaddon receives his dowry, he automatically gives up his conjugal rights toward his wife for the duration of the relationship with the warlock. She yearned to be in the arms of a man with flesh and blood.

"Are you sure Santiago Montoya?" Angelique asked excitedly.

"I am, as long as you are Angelique Sakola. I think we have something here worth exploring, don't you?"

"I do too. Are you aware he might ask for something totally crazy?"

"Don't you worry about that reina, I am ready for him. So, is that a yes?" queried Santiago holding her chin with his finger and looking straight into her eyes.

"Yes, yes it is," shouted Angelique throwing both her arms around Santiago's neck "Let's do this!"

Words could not describe how excited she was. She was really fond of Santiago. She believed that if there was a man who could deal with anything Abaddon would throw his way, that would be Santiago. She had such a good feeling about him.

They spent some time making plans and trying to anticipate Abaddon's reaction to their romance over a glass of wine and a cheeseboard. Then, to avoid falling into temptation Santiago passionately kissed Angelique before leaving. While their tongues intertwined Angelique enjoyed a foretaste of the passion that laid ahead with Santiago. Hot and flustered after his departure, she consoled herself with Mexican soap operas and popcorn that night.

Chapter 24
Ludovic and Erika

"Over here Ludovic!"

"Erika, Erika over your shoulder!"

There was no doubt in Ludovic's mind that someone at the club must have tipped off the press. A frenzy of paparazzi in search of celebrity snaps crowded Ludovic and Erika like a pack of wolves as they stepped out of the club. The couple were faced with a barrage of flashing camera lights and over-zealous reporters and would not have been able to walk through had it not been for the intervention of the venue's bouncers who kept the reporters at bay.

Ludovic Galant abhorred any kind of media interference with his private life. It was that side to fame he still had not warmed to in his six-year career as a premier league football player. Erika on the other hand secretly welcomed the attention she was drawing upon herself since she began dating the French Dulwich FC striker. She had hopes it would give her stagnant modelling career a boost and even open doors to the film industry.

It was around twelve midnight when Ludovic and Erika left the 'Panther' nightclub. The exclusive club located in Soho, London, was the hosting venue for Ludovic's team championship victory celebratory party. As the couple walked on, some persistent journalists kept pace with them, taking snaps, some offering their congratulations to Ludovic for his team's win whilst others, more inquisitive, probed into their personal lives by firing more intrusive questions.

"We heard you got engaged. Has Ludovic put a ring on it Erika?" yelled one of them.

"Come on Erika, is it true?" badgered another reporter.

Erika smiled timidly, nervously slipped her side blonde fringe behind her ear, holding on tightly to Ludovic's upper arm.

They quickly marched toward Ludovic's Aston Martin Vanquish. Erika, secretly harboured the hope that Ludovic might pop the question very soon. The press got wind that Ludovic had taken a trip to the jeweller recently – hence the inquisition about the state of their relationship – unbeknownst to them the purpose for the visit to the jeweller was to purchase a pair of diamond earrings which he gave to Erika for her birthday. She would have hastily exchanged the earrings for an engagement ring any day. Their romance was kindled over a year ago and they were counted among the most glamorous celebrity couples in showbiz; the handsome footballer and his drop-dead gorgeous model girlfriend. She was crazy about Ludovic and convinced he was the love of her life. She could hardly wait for the time he would ask for her hand in marriage. That ring on her finger would make her the envy of many women.

Hailed a sex symbol by numerous women magazines, Ludovic was French Caribbean with a fair caramel complexion and light brown eyes. He was about six foot four inches, slender with an extremely toned physique. His soft afro hair was his trademark which at times he'd let loose in a light kinky sexy style and, at other times, he would sport them in twists. In addition, to beating his fellow players to the title of football personality of the year three years in a row, Ludovic was also regarded as a fashion icon thanks to his versatile dress sense; he had the ability to look stellar suited-up, combined with a knack for making the most basic of sportswear items look superb. He regularly modelled for elite prêt à porter fashion designers and top of the range sports gear manufacturers.

Once inside the car, Erika grabbed Ludovic's head and planted a kiss on his lips predominantly for the benefit of the paparazzis who surrounded the Aston Martin taking pictures.

"I love you," whispered Erika to Ludovic as she leaned back on the passenger.

Ludovic was not oblivious to Erika's underlying motives and was quite annoyed that by her actions she was fostering the rumour that marriage might be on the cards. This kiss she had just given him was bound to be front page news in the tabloids the following day. Ludovic was not ready to get married and even less so to Erika. He was already starting to get bored of her. She was far too needy and strange. There was something dark about her which he had to admit at times was scary. He had even begun to suspect whether she was involved in some weird sect. Hence, he was in the process of devising the best way to end the relationship, which was a far cry from the press wedding predictions.

Erika on the other hand was buzzing and had begun to believe that wedding bells were definitely on the horizon.

Ludovic seemed as keen as her when she kissed him in front of the press. The very thought of becoming Mrs Ludovic Galant got her so horny that she could hardly wait until they arrived at her rented penthouse in South Kensington to have a quickie with her beau.

Ludovic's intention was to drop Erika and drive off. He needed some rest because he had training the following day, but she insisted he escorted her into the penthouse, hoping to lure him into spending the night. They had barely set foot inside the apartment where Erika put her arms around Ludovic and seductively teased his ear lobe with her moist tongue before working her way onto his lips while her hands began to unzip his trousers. Ludovic attributed Erika's sexual urges to the 'Dom Perignon White Gold Jeroboam' champagne she had been drinking all night. He knew Erika to be rather subtle and discreet in her sexual advances. She was not the type to initiate sex quite so openly and boldly. The only time she would be this forward was when intoxicated. Regardless of the reason behind her seductive advances, Ludovic was getting hot under the collar. As she groped his crotch, he figured he could spare five minutes to give the lady what she wanted. After all, she was very provocative and wild when drunk.

He responded to her enticing kiss by pinning her against the wall. Ludovic's fingers were halfway through lifting up Erika's little black dress when the hallway lights came on. Stopping in their tracks to see who was the person that turned on the lights, they saw Carla's head peeking out of the living room door with one hand on the light switch.

"Hey, love birds," she said with a cheeky grin before disappearing back into the living room.

Erika's amorous intent was short-lived. Extremely annoyed, she nervously pulled down her dress giving Ludovic the most apologetic look, "I am sorry I didn't know she was coming today. Let's just go into the bedroom," she proposed.

The moment was lost. Ludovic was no longer interested. Zipping up his trousers he replied, "I have training tomorrow, I am going to use the toilet, then leave." He disappeared in the bathroom which was situated in the apartment corridor. A dejected Erika picked up her purse which she had dropped on the floor during her clinch with Ludovic and joined Carla in the sitting room. She would have killed her without so much blinking an eyelid had she not been her sister.

"How come you did not tell me you were coming?" questioned Erika.

Without looking at Erika, Carla kept flicking through a Forbes magazine. "I did, sister dear. Check your text messages. Besides I live here too, and don't have to ask for your permission whenever I want to show up," retorted Carla.

Erika grabbed her purse and pulled out her phone. Carla was not lying, she did send a couple of text messages.

"I am waiting for your apologies," mocked Carla.

"Whatever... you spoiled things for me, you idiot," mumbled Erika, hitting her sister with one of the sofa cushions.

"Get ready because things might just get worse," warned Carla dodging her sister's blow. As if ruining a night of love-making with Ludovic was not bad enough, Carla had some unwelcome news about the last person Erika wanted to hear about: Angelique Sakola. She shoved the magazine in Erika's face.

Erika read out loud; "Meet Angelique Sakola, one of the world's top influential females. Young, charming and intelligent, Angelique is an inspiration to young bankers aspiring to reach the highest echelon in the banking industry. Since her appointment as the CEO of WAXXA, Angelique has succeeded where her predecessors previously failed."

Infuriated, Erika cut short the reading of the article and tossed the publication in the air "blah blah blah... she is a stupid woman".

"Even the Times is talking about that stupid woman. The world seems captivated with stupidity by the look of things," Carla commented sarcastically to her sister. She slammed the publication onto the table and picked up her smart phone and started going through social media.

"I was having a beautiful evening until now," sighed Erika when they both heard the door in the corridor bang.

"It sounds like your boyfriend has just left," said Carla.

"I can't believe he didn't even say goodbye."

"Charming!!" sneered Carla.

"It's all your fault for interrupting! I'll have to make it up to him. I need that ring on my finger before the end of the year."

"So you believe he'll propose then?" asked Carla.

Erika pointed her index finger in the air and boasted, "You see this little finger dearest sister – I have got Ludovic wrapped all around it. He won't escape me."

"You sound wickedly confident. Have you made the blood covenant yet?"

"Not yet, I don't want him to suspect a thing when I do it. I am trying to figure out how I can get his blood and make him drink mine."

"I wouldn't delay if I were you," cautioned Carla.

"You're right, I have decided it'll be done this week," vowed Erika.

"Fab! I think we should toast to your coming marriage," proposed Carla.

Walking over to the mini bar, she opened the fridge and took out a bottle of champagne and popped out the cork. After handing a flute to her sister, Carla raised hers and proposed a toast:

"To the future Mrs Ludovic Galant!"

"To the future Mrs Ludovic Galant!" echoed Erika.

"Such a waste of a hard on," grumbled Ludovic as he anticipated the stiffness would appease as he took a leak. He had decided he would say a quick goodbye to the girls and head home, sticking to his original plan for an early night. Upon exiting the bathroom, an unexpected strong northerly wind blew from the opened window causing the door to slam with a loud bang. Walking toward the living room to apologise to the girls about the loud noise, he overheard Erika whinge about him leaving without saying goodbye. On the verge of going inside the room to reassure his girlfriend he had not left, he stopped in his tracks by the door, his curiosity aroused when he inadvertently overheard Erika mention wanting the ring around her finger. Unable to help himself he ended up eavesdropping on their entire conversation. As the girls began toasting on the marriage with Ludovic, he tiptoed toward the main door and left quietly closing the door behind him.

Ludovic was stunned by what he had discovered, especially Erika's intention of making a blood covenant with him, without his knowledge or consent. He suspected Erika before of belonging to some sects, now he had the proof she was definitely involved in some occult practices and her along with her family relatives were a bunch of weirdos. One thing for sure, he did not like the idea of swapping blood with her or anybody else. He had to act fast to end this madness.

Chapter 25
Woman Scorned

It was seven a.m. and Erika was on her knees with her head buried in the toilet bowl for the past fifteen minutes. A pounding headache and a nauseous feeling caused by an epic hangover cut short Erika's sleep. She could not control the urge to throw up. Her entire body was shivering, covered in cold sweat. This was not a new experience by far. Champagne just did not agree with her and she was fully aware of it. Unfortunately for her, her palate had a strong inclination toward the luxurious bubbly nectar.

Cursing herself and vowing not to touch a drop of champagne for as long as she lived, she crawled back to bed. It was then she heard a ping, it was a text message. At first, she could hardly believe what she was reading. Her hangover was suddenly gone, she was livid and in a state of panic. She had to show this to Carla, she needed reassurance that she was not hallucinating. Carla's bedroom was empty and her bed done. The younger of the sisters could handle her alcohol better than the older, notwithstanding that she also suffered a serious case of insomnia. Erika found her in the kitchen drinking a cup of black coffee. Erika was as pale as a white sheet causing Carla to be anxious at the sight of her sister, "Erika what's going on? If you weren't a witch I would say you look like you have seen a ghost!"

"Read this!" ordered Erika handing the phone over to her sister. After reading the text, Carla returned the phone to her sister, perplexed, "What kind of nonsense is this?"

The text was a break-up message from Ludovic; 'Hi Erika, we are over. I am sorry but I'm not feeling this anymore and I'm not ready for a long-term relationship. Let's stay friends. Sorry, Ludovic'.

"Please tell me this is not happening," wept Erika.

Erika's life had taken a major turn of events. One minute she was convinced she was about to walk down the aisle with Ludovic and the next he was breaking up with her via text message. She did not see this coming and was left in the dark about his reasons for dumping her.

Various attempts to reach Ludovic by phone proved unfruitful later that day. He was not picking up her calls. Even after she tried using a different number the outcome was the same. It was as if he had changed his mobile number altogether. He went as far as unfriending her on his social media networks and changed his status to single. Erika felt insulted and humiliated by his sudden disdain for her which in her opinion was unfounded and undeserved.

Three weeks into the split, she suffered a severe case of depression and attempted to take her own life. Unable to cope with her sister's grief, Carla called Greta who flew to London as soon as she was alerted to her elder daughter's condition. Greta held her frail daughter in her arms every night while she laid in bed. Her mother's heart was breaking. She had already lost her husband and she was not ready to lose her daughter. She took it upon herself to motivate her daughter.

"Honey, you are an extremely powerful witch. If you love

this boy so much, use your powers and go get him!" urged Greta.

"Mum, I wanted him to love me by his own will like he did and use as little magic as possible. I want true love mum…" It was the most exhilarating feeling for Erika to be wanted without having to manipulate her way into what she desired through witchcraft. Her mother was suggesting a more powerful, darker and deeper method of magic which would bind Ludovic's soul and make him her love slave forever.

Greta persisted in her argument, "Often in life things don't always come in the perfect format we want them to, but as long as you want it. Then that's the only thing that matters. So it is within your powers to get it, go get it!"

Erika was forced to admit her mother had a valid point. She wanted Ludovic more than anything else in the whole world. So what if it was not the perfect reciprocal love she had imagined? Even if it was one-sided she wanted him and decided to follow her mother's advice to use her stronger powers to make Ludovic fall in love with her for eternity.

"Greta!" Erika and Carla had a habit of addressing their mother by her first name whenever they came to an important decision, "You are as cunning as a fox. You win! I'll go get Ludovic back!" swore Erika.

"That's my girl!" clapped Greta proudly. "Let me know when and if you need any help."

As they began to plan their move, Erika recalled she had a commitment that would delay her plans. She explained to Greta that she had a lovers' bond with the merman king of the Göta älv-Klarälven river which was binding for the next eighteen months. As long as that bond was in force, it was unlawful for Erika to join herself to another man through an everlasting love spell – which was Erika's intention. The lovers' bond signified that Erika was the legitimate wife of the merman king in the underworld. Their union however had a time span which once reached Erika would be free to unite to another in the underworld which was what she planned to do with Ludovic.

Greta lifted up her daughter's spirit, "It's only a setback, you'll just have to be patient. Eighteen months will pass in no time."

After that pep talk with her mum, Erika cheered up and was filled with a new wicked joie de vivre. Ludovic did not stand a chance against her. That very thought brought a slow lingering witch's maleficent smile to her face.

Chapter 26
The Dowry

Every three years, on the thirteenth day of the thirteenth week in the thirteenth month of the mystic lunar calendar the underworld would celebrate the feast of fertility. Citizens of the underworld gathered in the capital, the city of Abaddon which was located underwater in the Bermuda triangle for the week-long festivity which paid homage to Abaddon's virility and sensuality. Warlocks, witches and creatures of the underworld travelled from every corner of the universe to indulge in nights of heavy drinking, substance abuse and orgies. As a goodwill gesture it was customary for Abaddon to free his wives to mate with other warlocks but only on strictly tight conditions. It was a once in a life-time opportunity for sages and powerful warlocks who were able to meet Abaddon's extravagant demands to acquire one of the ruler's wives as theirs for either a night or a longer period of time depending on their capabilities. Out of Abaddon's wives, Angelique was one of the most popular, bright with looks to match. It was not surprising that requests for her sexual favours were extremely high, especially considering that the thirteenth month of the mystic lunar calendar only occurred every three years. However, despite the level of interest she generated none of the candidates had thus far succeeded in winning her due to Abaddon's possessiveness. He had ways to ensure that their fantasy of Angelique remained unattainable. For instance, a few years back Abaddon challenged petitioners to an arm wrestle offering Angelique as a prize to the winner. Needless to say, there were no challengers that year.

This year was different and Santiago knew it. Abaddon was unusually distracted with his latest wife, the striking princess and priestess Malaika, daughter of King Shahrukh of the Hindustani kingdom located in the southern part of India. So captivating was Princess Malaika's beauty that she had monopolised Abaddon's attention since her arrival to the detriment of his other wives, including Angelique. For that reason Santiago had a strong feeling Abaddon would be more generous and lenient than he had been in the past with requests for Angelique. He had total confidence in his powers to not only secure a successful outcome to his petition but to also blow out of the water any rising competitor.

Petitions for Abaddon's wives, except for Malaika who was not yet available, were counted on the third day of the feast. The announcement of Abaddon's conditions, known as the Abaddon's dowry, was a ceremonious matter and took place in his palace, in the largest audience hall; the throne room. There was nothing remotely comparable to Abaddon's throne room in the physical realm. At the entrance of the hall stood two tall silver statues of half man, half goat creatures. The throne room itself was decorated with embroidered purple and gold tapestries. A few hundred feet above the marble floor, an imposing display of canvas of worshiping cherubs rendering homage to Abaddon, draped the ceiling providing the perfect background to crystal chandeliers.

Abaddon sat on his throne chair made of pure gold which had two bulls standing beside the chair's armrests. The top of the throne was the gold head of a bull with his horns pointed upward, symbolising Abaddon in all his glory. The throne had thirteen golden steps. The members of the council of the sages sat on thirteen thrones at the foot of the stairs to the right, whilst Abaddon's eight wives sat to the left. At the thirteenth hour, the royal speaker opened the dowry session. After rendering homage to Abaddon all the petitioners for Abaddon's wives were bid to stand and cite the name of the spouse of their choice. It came as no surprise that Angelique received the most requests, much to Santiago's annoyance. This was just the beginning of the process. The follow-up stage was Abaddon's unveiling of his dowry, after which the would-be-suitors would declare whether they wished to pursue or forfeit depending on their confidence in meeting Abaddon's demands. In the final stage, Abaddon's queen's approval would be sought. She would make a public declaration confirming whether or not she welcomed her admirers request for love and select one if there were many.

Santiago was not the only one to be annoyed with Angelique's army of admirers. Abaddon was hacked off to hear the name of Santiago among the petitioners. It annoyed him even further because this was the first time one of his sages was going through this process and Santiago would not have put himself forward unless he had fallen for his Angelique and vice versa. The thought of Angelique being in love with someone and especially one so close displeased Abaddon deeply. He had promised himself to be reasonable with his dowry this year, but felt a sudden change of heart.

When the time to reveal the dowry for his brides came,

Abaddon arose. After basking in the cheers and praises from the audience he proclaimed with a strong voice, "My fellow subjects, today I want to demonstrate my generosity and announce that the dowry for each of my brides is a soul for one hundred and eighty days!" People clapped as Abaddon continued, "However for my lovely dove's eyes Angelique I request five hundred thousand souls for one hundred and eighty days." Deep silence fell in the throne room following that statement, so much so that one could hear a fly flap its wings.

Angelique gasped in shock. Santiago was startled, he got it wrong. This year was the worse. Abaddon had made his feelings loud and clear about anybody approaching Angelique.

The ruler of the underworld returned to his seat whilst the palace speaker stepped on stage and invited those wishing to pursue their quest following the announcement of the dowry to stand.

Whilst a couple of contenders stood up for Abaddon's spouses: Ariana and Sheila. Santiago exchanged a desperate look with Angelique as he pondered on what his next move ought to be. five hundred thousand souls was such a major undertaking that none of Angelique's other candidates dared to stand up. Fixing his eyes unto Angelique's eyes across the throne, Santiago realised he wanted her more than anything else in the world and was ready to do what it takes to have her. This time not even Abaddon would stand in his way. In a leap of faith and to Abaddon's and the gathering's amazement Santiago rose from his seat.

All eyes were on Santiago, the crowd could not believe

what they were witnessing. What happened next was even more astonishing. Angelique stepped down from her royal seat, walked past the throne's steps toward Santiago. Following a long gaze, as if they were alone in the room. Angelique pulled out a pair of small scissors from her small purse, cut off a lock of her long curly raven jet black mane and placed it in Santiago's hand. This signified she approved his petition. The crowd went into a frenzy, hailing Santiago and Angelique as protagonists of the ultimate modern day love story. Abaddon exploded inwardly.

As the crowd cheered, a conflicted Santiago thought within himself 'either I am suicidal or totally loco for this woman or both'. Failure to pay a dowry often resulted in severe punishment, being a sage he had much to lose should he fail to comply.

Abaddon vigorously snapped his hands to put an end to the tumult.

"Well, well," he said after the hall had gone quiet. "What do we have here, Santiago Montoya, Angelique's knight in shining armour?" he added with a hint of sarcasm.

Abaddon had no choice but to extend his golden snake shaped sceptre toward Santiago from his seat, "Very well then, sage Montoya. five hundred thousand souls it is. You have no more than thirteen days to honour your pledge!"

Both Ariana and Sheila were consumed with envy at Abaddon's blatant favouritism toward Angelique. Their dowry requests resembled a meagre copper coin compared to that of Angelique. Therefore, when it came to their turn to acknowledge the requests made for their favours, feeling insulted they resorted to rejecting all their candidates.

A few days following the feast, the reality and seriousness of his pledge began to dawn on Santiago. He had an almost impossible task ahead of him. To bring half a million souls was no small matter, it was the equivalent of wiping out an entire town. Extensive magical powers would be required, even for an accomplished warlock such as Santiago, which would drain him of all his powers and make him vulnerable to his enemies. As such, he was glad when Angelique dropped by for a surprise visit at his hotel room in London, where he was staying for a few days on a drug cartel related business trip. She was fully aware of his predicament and had come to offer her help since there were no rules against it. What Santiago was unaware of was that she had already worked out a plan.

For his part, Santiago was pleasantly surprised to see Angelique standing at the door of his five-star hotel suite. She looked youthful in a pair of skinny jeans, high black boots and a knitted roll neck top. Her innocent smile, with her hair pulled back in a ponytail revealing her perfect bone structure was an open invitation for Santiago to steal a passionate smooch from her. The tingling sensation of her tongue caressing his was a reminder and a promise to Santiago of what awaited him should he be successful in honouring the dowry pledge. His lust for Angelique was like a slow burning fire intensifying with each passing day. Their attraction for one another was electrifying, he was not sure how long he could resist making love to her. He felt he was going insane. Luckily for his sanity, she had a plan to help him secure the half million souls requested by Abaddon, hence hastening their union. It was deviously elaborated, it left Santiago speechless. He loved it!

ISABELLE KAMALANDWA BRYAN

Chapter 27
Tragedy for Love

In his ten-year career as a news correspondent Anthony Cedarcourt had yet to witness a devastation of the size he experienced in the island of Guyane Sud. He and his crew had to urgently take the first flight from Haiti where they were covering a volcanic eruption to the capital city of Guyane Sud, Ville-de-Mère, after receiving news that one of the deadliest earthquakes known to man had hit the small Caribbean island. Anthony was physically and emotionally exhausted, he missed home. He was hoping that his quick stopover at the neighbouring island of Haiti would be the last for a while following a long streak of overseas reportages. He was looking forward to returning to Surrey in England to spend some family time with his wife and their newborn baby girl, whose birth he had missed due to the demands of his job with STCW News.

However, nothing could have prepared him for the trail of devastation the forces of nature left behind in the beautiful paradise like French island. The entire city of Ville-de-Mère was engulfed by an earthquake of a never heard before ten magnitude overnight. Anthony 's tiredness gave way to shock. As they walked through the city, the scene was distressingly apocalyptic, straight out of a horror movie. The damage was incalculable, across the city were collapsed houses and buildings, dark grey smoke from fire caused by the breaks on gas and power lines and dust from smashed concrete clouded the once clear blue skies. Bodies of humans and animals alike lay motionless on the city's wreckages amidst the tumult of frantic and overwhelmed emergency services. The town was in mourning, some desperately looking for their lost ones, others having accepted the tragedy wept uncontrollably. Wishing not to violate the privacy of the grieving survivors, Anthony sought no interviews, but rather asked his cameraman to silently film the desolate state of the Ville-de-Mère in the aftermath of what came to be known as earthquake Lucinda.

About twenty minutes into the filming, Anthony's attention was inexplicably drawn to a figure, it was that of a young afro-Caribbean woman, crouched down in the middle of rubble of what probably used to be the living room of a house. She was quietly rocking back and forth. Sensing the close presence of Anthony, she turned her face and looked intensely at Anthony. Her soft curly afro hair was disheveled, parts of her face were covered in dark dust, yet her green eyes filled with grief were so striking that Anthony signalled his crew to follow him and to keep rolling the camera as he approached this young woman. As Anthony got closer she turned away, rested her face on her knees and carried on rocking back and forth.

Anthony felt sympathy for this young woman, and touched her on her shoulder and asked in his elementary French;

"Mademoiselle, on peut vous aider?"

"You English?" she asked.

"Yes, I am an English journalist. I am profoundly sorry for your loss."

"This earthquake, no accident... This earthquake no accident" she repeated as she rocked back and forth faster, fixating her eyes intensely straight into nothing.

Anthony was intrigued and wondered whether she was utilising the incorrect English words or whether she was undergoing a traumatic episode.

She carried on, " yesterday... the sky very very dark... big wind... one man and one woman flying in the sky wearing black . Woman long black hair... she and man witch... earthquake no accident... earthquake no accident..."

Anthony was unsure about how to respond to her or how to take that information. The people of Guyane Sud were well known for their superstitious nature. But attributing an earthquake, which is a scientifically proven natural phenomena, to the paranormal did not register well with Anthony's pragmatic mind. There was nothing Anthony could do, but he empathised with this young woman's pain and loss.

"This is such a tragedy and again I am sorry. Here is my card and you can contact me if you ever need any help." As she made no attempt to take the card he held out to her, he placed it beside her on the dusty floor and walked away.

On the plane back to England, he drafted his final report confirming that five hundred thousand lives were claimed by earthquake Lucinda. For some reason, he still could not shake out of his head the image of this Creole woman with no name. Who was she and why on earth did he give her his card?

The following day, in the capital city of the netherworld, Santiago entered the courts of Abaddon triumphant. Bowing before the throne he declared, "Hail master

Abaddon, the dowry you requested for Angelique has been paid."

From his throne seat Abaddon nonchalantly brought his palms together at the sight of Santiago kneeling before him and gave him a satirical standing ovation that reverberated around the walls of the throne room. "Humans, humans," he muttered, "you will never cease to amaze me. You'd go to such extreme lengths to conquer a woman. I wonder if this is what you people call love?" He paused for a brief moment in deep thought and then carried on, "I knew a man once, thousands of years ago, who died for love. How foolish." he mumbled. For millennia Abaddon observed how this feeling called love had been the root cause of pain, strife, wars, jealousy, murders and heartbreaks in humans. Yet it puzzled him, how equally it provided such a feeling of bliss in men that they'd be willing to front death for it. There were times, he would have desired to experience love, but, alas, that was a gift to humans and not soulless creatures. The one thing that has always frustrated him with humans was love. He could handle greed, anger, hate, lust but love has evaded him in every corner. He has fought many battles since the beginning and his greatest defeat unknown to his subjects was against love. Even though he was unable to determine whether Santiago and Angelique were in love, he still felt that familiar feeling of defeat as he handed Angelique over to Santiago for the agreed period of six months.

At last, the lovers were free to yield to the burning desire they had long suppressed. In a honeymoon style vacation, Santiago whisked Angelique to the idyllic tropical planet of 'El Santiago' in the cosmos. The beautiful palm tree planet which bore his name was a gift from Abaddon for his knighthood. Out there in the astral world, alone, they consummated their insane attraction for one another undisturbed and without inhibition. It was magical.

ISABELLE KAMALANDWA BRYAN

Chapter 28
No Weapon Formed

Angelique could hardly believe what was coming out of Jen's mouth. They both sat in Angelique's office where Jen was reporting on the outcome of the operation to take over Ndeko mines. What was inconceivable to Angelique was not primarily that the seven hundred and forty eight militia group had failed to take over Ndeko mines, but the manner by which they had failed. This was of the strangest nature, even for Angelique who is well versed in magic and the supernatural. She was baffled.

According to Jen, at the operation's first attempt, general Mbuyi, the leader of the seven hundred and forty eight militia group, was so confident it would be an easy operation that he only sent a small number of his soldiers to besiege Ndeko mines. He had construed that because the coverage of Ndeko mines was along a stretch of land equivalent to three small villages, about thirty soldiers would suffice. Besides, to their knowledge, only unarmed civilians worked at Ndeko. He also did not feel the need for a libabe to accompany the soldiers. He had assessed that a bunch of unarmed civilians were very unlikely to put up any sort of resistance.

The assault was scheduled in the daytime so that Ndeko administrative staff could be taken hostage and coerced to sign papers agreeing to continue working in the mines under the militia regime. The first strangest thing was that the militia had difficulty localising Ndeko mines. The site where the GPS led them to was just some bare empty land. There was no one there, apart from a woman who, according to Jen, fitted Rachel Parker's description standing in the middle of the wasteland. She was alone, wearing matching grey trousers and jacket. Her auburn hair was pulled in a ponytail. She looked delicate and yet there was an authority about her as she stood in her full five foot three inch height.

The soldiers were puzzled to see this western Caucasian woman alone in such an inhospitable environment. The sun was at its peak, it was scorching hot. The captain asked her who she was and what she was doing there. Ignoring their question she spoke to them with an authoritative voice, "Return where you came from, you will not find what you are looking for."

"What do you know about what we are looking for?" challenged the leader of the group.

"I know you are looking for Ndeko mines, you won't find it," she retorted.

At that point the leader raised and pointed his machine gun at Rachel. "What do you know? Speak or I'll kill you right here!' he ordered.

Rachel stared at him defiantly, "No weapon formed against me shall prosper. I strike you all with blindness!"

As soon as these words came out of her mouth a mist fell on all the soldiers' eyes, and they could no longer see and they stumbled about trying to find their way back to the camp.

A handful of soldiers managed to get back to the camp with the help of some kind-hearted villagers they encountered along the way. Upon hearing the soldiers' accounts of the event, general Mbuyi ordered a second takeover attempt. But this time, he was fronting the operation himself with one hundred soldiers and taking along the libabe to tackle any paranormal incidents.

Identical to the previous operation, as they drove for the destination of Ndeko mines, the GPS led them to the same waste land location. It was exactly the same scenario, there she was again, that western woman, standing in the middle of the waste land. Stepping out of his jeep, General Mbuyi asked her, "Are you the woman who made my soldiers blind?"

She ignored his question and said with the same authoritative voice, "If you are here looking for what they were looking for, you won't find it!"

'Woman, I advise you not to stand in our way. Where are the Ndeko mines?' barked General Mbuyi.

Rachel sniggered, "Don't you have Google map, street map? Why are you asking me?"

General Mbuyi was getting aggravated and slightly startled. This was an abnormal situation. However, he was no stranger to the paranormal and there was no way he was about to let a foreign Caucasian woman get the better of him in his own country. "Stop playing games, you are outnumbered and in case you try one of your blindness tricks we have another type of friend."

The libabe who until then had been invisible revealed himself so that all could see him. His sight was terrifying, including to General Mbuyi's men.

Rachel took a slight step back at the sight of the libabe, but did not flinch and retorted, "Today your eyes won't go blind, on the contrary, they will be open so you can see that those that are with me are greater than your soldiers and this soulless creature you dragged along with you."

Upon Rachel's words their eyes opened up and they saw a multitude of eight-foot tall men dressed in shiny silver white apparel appear. There were so many that they covered the entire wasteland. They had the appearance of warriors. They wore breastplates, and held a shield on the left hand and a long thick sword on the right. They surrounded Rachel on all sides. Their presence generated such radiating light that Mbuyi and his men had to shield their eyes with their hands. The libabe began to shriek uncontrollably in the presence of these warriors.

Then the chief warrior descended from the sky, he was clothed in a cloud, with a rainbow above his head; his face was like the sun, and his legs were like bronze. He spoke up, his voice sounded like the roar of a lion, "Mbuyi take your men and do not attempt an assault against Ndeko Corporation again, or it shall not go well with you!" Mbuyi and his men could not withstand the glare emanating from these celestial creatures, they were on their knees hiding their faces. The chief warrior turned to the Libabe and pointed a finger at the creature, "You have broken the law! Seize him!" he ordered. Two warriors launched forward at an incredible speed, apprehended the libabe and dragged him into an unseen world. Upon the disappearance of the libabe General Mbuyi and his men, overtaken by uncontrollable fear, dispersed, each seeking to run as far away as possible from that place.

Holding her head with both hands, Angelique was in panic mode.

"This is just crazy. Where is the libabe now?" she enquired.

"Gone. I am sorry, that libabe has not been seen since," replied Jen apologetically.

Angelique knew that if she was in trouble before, now she was in double trouble. Abaddon will never forgive her the loss of a libabe. They were his soldiers, his babies and he valued every single one of them. There was only a limited number of libabes in the underworld because they could not procreate. Therefore, any that went missing or were somehow destroyed, could not be replaced. It will be just a matter of time before Abaddon finds out that the libabe is missing. She had to find a solution before Abaddon gets wind of this.

This is a complete and utter disaster, thought Angelique, Oh crap!

ISABELLE KAMALANDWA BRYAN

Chapter 29
Old Allies

Looking at the amazing view of the city of London from her top floor office at WAXXA building, Angelique questioned how when one area of her life picks up, another has to take a dive down. Why could not her love and professional lives evolve in the same direction?

Things could not be sweeter on the love front. A few weeks into her relationship with Santiago, had she been a cartoon character, she'll be singing with the swallows and dancing with squirrels. The feelings and the wave of emotions incited by this relationship were that intense. Santiago was just like her, he got her, he understood her. Being with him was effortless and beautiful. It was a welcome change from Abaddon, nothing could compare to the warmth of a real full-blooded man.

Maybe the universe does not permit excessive happiness and has a way of keeping us grounded Angelique thought. On one hand she was soaring in love and on the other sinking in business. The Ndeko dossier was a head sore, a thorn in her side.

Conscious she was running fast out of time, Angelique needed to act fast. The priority was to ensure that Abaddon did not suspect anything was wrong. In that respect she gave Jen strict orders not to mention the takeover failure nor the disappearance of the libabe to anyone. Secondly, she needed answers and knew exactly what to do. Once a year, as part of her duty as chief of tribe , Angelique had to congregate with elders of the

Tumbu village to perform rituals and offer sacrifices to the underworld. That time of the year had arrived and while in Congo she was going to grab the opportunity to visit an old friend. She picked up her phone and summoned her secretary into her office, "Amanda, please ask the pilot to get the plane ready, I am flying out to Congo today. Thanks!"

Before she even knocked on the wooden door Angelique heard Ma'Dika's voice "Come on in Angelique. I was expecting you."

It had never crossed Angelique's mind that she would ever set foot in that damp shack again. It had not changed neither had Ma'Dika. She still smelt funky and Angelique's attempts at avoiding a hug from the old lady were to no avail. Following the awkward hug, Ma'Dika invited Angelique to take a seat on one of the stools and offered Angelique a drink, some type of concoction, which she politely declined.

As Angelique was about to get into the purpose of her visit, Ma'Dika spoke first, "The spirits told me you were coming. I sense your soul is heavy my child."

Angelique let out a big sigh, "You are right, I am working on the deal to take over a mining company in the Kasai region and I am encountering opposition from a woman named Rachel Parker Ndeko. I have no clue how to overcome her, but I need her out of my way. If I don't succeed, I dread what Abaddon would do to me. You are the only one I can turn to for help."

Angelique shared with Ma'Dika the details about her failed mission to take over Ndeko mines. After listening attentively, Ma'Dika picked up a wooden black pipe which she inhaled deeply, before blowing out the smoke. Carefully observing the shapes of the smoke in the air, she began declaring her divination, "Rachel Parker Ndeko is a very strong and dangerous opponent. She stands in front of you like an iron pillar and bronze wall. She won't be shaken, she is as fierce as a lioness. She moves like the wind, you cannot tell where she comes from or where she is going."

This is far from what Angelique wanted to hear. She wanted solutions not additional challenges.

"I hear she is not a witch. What kind of powers does she possess?" enquired an alarmed Angelique.

Ma'Dika continued her divination, "She is not a witch, she is like the wind. I see a hedge of fire surrounding her. To defeat her you will need to break the hedge."

Angelique grew more aggravated by the cryptic and hidden nature of Ma'Dika's language. "What's that hedge and how do I break it to defeat her?" she queried.

"It is not going to be easy. However, I see she is well versed in the supernatural and is no stranger to mysticism. You can fight her in that realm using your dark magic powers."

"Finally getting somewhere. This is a language I understand. Am I not the best in my craft in this entire universe? She will experience the full extent of my wrath. I won't mess about, I'll go for the kill," proclaimed Angelique.

In light of Angelique's exuberance, Ma'Dike cautioned her, "Rachel is a mighty adversary. If you don't defeat her, she will be the end of you."

ISABELLE KAMALANDWA BRYAN

Chapter 30
Intel Is Key

"Come on Jen, cheer up!" Mei was trying her best to lift up her friend's mood, "it's gonna be fun!"

Jen was definitely not in the mood to attend a reunion party. She has had the worst day of her life and was anxious about her future. The Ndeko takeover was a big deal, a make or break. Right now the break was so close she could smell it. With her life and career hanging in the balance, she would have rather opted for a night in to figure out her next move, instead of dancing the night way. She had faith in Angelique's capacity to somehow turn things around, but it was not in her character to surrender her fate into someone else's hands. Being the master of her own destiny had always been Jen's dictum.

The thought of Abaddon catching wind of the hole they were in filled her with dread. Abaddon knew no mercy, she hated to imagine what his reaction would be. But hard pressed by Mei's nagging combined with the fact that this event was planned for a while, Jen finally gave in and agreed to go to the party. They strolled past through the small streets of central London to the Hilton Hotel in Marble Arch where the London Business School alumni reunion bash was being held. The noise of their stilettos echoed in the night as they walked hastily in their cocktail black mini dresses.

Mei detected that her friend's countenance was still sombre and endeavoured to liven her up and contaminate her with her own excitement about the night out.

"Don't worry hun, whatever happened at work today forget about it. Let's drink champagne tonight and have fun."

"Mei, I have had a major setback in an extremely important deal today! My boss and I could be in serious trouble," grumbled Jen. Mei was a lovely girl and a good friend, but she was not involved in the underworld, therefore could not possibly understand the gravity of Jen's situation nor was there anything she could do about it anyway. Notwithstanding, Jen was really fond of Mei, she was her closest friend. They met while studying at the London Business School, since they were the only two Chinese girls in the Msc in the Financial Derivatives course that year, they bonded straight away and struck a friendship which had lasted since.

"I hear you Jen, but worrying about it will not change anything. Besides you told my boss that Angelique is one tough cookie. I am sure she'll pull through," reassured Mei as they reached the venue.

Ryan, the reunion organizer, welcomed them at the door with flutes of effervescent champagne. A private equity manager in a London-based investment bank , Ryan was always the heart and soul of parties. Dating back from university years Ryan would throw the wildest parties on campus. He was very popular, a larger than life guy with an icky sense of humour that often targeted women's buttocks and breasts. When Jen heard that he actually had a girlfriend, she felt sorry for the woman. In her mind only a total moron would put up with that misogynist.

"Hey, pretty ladies. Welcome to the reunion of the year! I am glad you could make it!." Ryan planted a wet kiss on both Jen and Mei's cheeks. He then called over a lovely tall brunette, he placed a firm hand on her waist saying, "Ladies, let me introduce to my girl, Carla. Carla, this is Jen and Mei."

The girls greeted each other with kisses on the cheeks.

"She is my assistant host and has a perfect set of melons," boasted Ryan cupping one of Carla's breasts and winking at the girls.

Jen did not expect any less from Ryan and simply rolled her eyes. Mei on the other hand released an embarrassed chuckle. She has had a soft spot for Ryan for as long as Jen could remember. Regrettably for Ryan, he never paid any attention to her probably because she was not dumb enough.

Being groped in public did not seem to bother Carla who was happy to reciprocate; she suggestively pinched his behind as he waltzed off to greet more incoming guests.

With Ryan gone, Carla stepped into her role of party assistant and attempted to make small talk with Jen and Mei, "So girls what do you do?"

"I am a Fund Manager at Society Management," replied Mei. Her eyes were hovering around the room, she could hardly wait to start mingling. She had already spotted a few people she wanted to go talk to. She was not interested in Carla. She had no recollection ever meeting her back on campus.

"I am chief of staff at WAXXA," replied Jen, 'What about you?"

Jen was curious about Carla, she sensed something rather familiar about Carla's aura but was having difficulty pinning it down. She was convinced she had seen her before, but could not pin where.

"Did we take some of the same classes at the Business School?" queried Jen.

Carla had to suppress a gasp when she heard about Jen's place of work. Like Jen, Carla also felt something familiar about Jen. The room was dark and Jen was wearing a long sleeve dress, so Carla could not check whether she had the invisible underworld tattoo. However, everything in her senses convinced her that Jen was a witch. It was well known in the underworld that WAXXA only employed underworld agents. Carla sipped her champagne to regain composure and kept her tattooed wrist out of sight, she was not about to blow the cover on her true identity.

"Wow WAXXA Bank, impressive. Humm, I am a model, never went to LBS. Ryan just wanted me to be here to help him organise the event," Carla clarified nonchalantly.

She must have seen her in some magazine which could justify why she seemed familiar, thought Jen.

"I do read a little about banks and stuff. Isn't the CEO of WAXXA this woman.. err... Angelique something?" probed Clara maliciously.

Jen was about to reply when Mei intervened, placing her arms around Jen, "Sorry Carla, I convinced Jen to come so that she'd forget about work. Her and her boss are not having the best of times with a very important deal at the moment. Jen is super stressed, so I really want her to think of nothing else except having a good time."

"I am sorry, of course," apologised Carla. "I have the perfect cure, let me introduce you to the best remedy for work trouble." She whistled at two of the most handsome young men across the room who made their way over.

"Ladies, meet Yuri and James, they are my friends and models," said Carla with a wink.

The boys were gorgeous, Yuri was half Japanese and half Danish and James was South African with beach blond hair and blue eyes. Mei suddenly lost the desire she had to mingle with old university friends and for a while Jen was happy to park the Ndeko takeover to one side. It turned out to be a great night for Jen and an even better morning waking up next to Yuri's perfectly toned body under her bed sheets.

On the other side of town, it was an equally good morning for Carla, albeit for a different reason. At the break of dawn, she got on the phone first thing to her mother, "Hi mum, it might turn out into a wild goose chase, but I heard something. Angelique is having some kind of trouble at WAXXA with a big deal she is working on. It might be worth doing some digging about it. Who knows it might just work in our favour to get back at this evil witch!"

ISABELLE KAMALANDWA BRYAN

Chapter 31
Abaddon's Threat

Angelique had a bad feeling as she walked into Abaddon's chambers slightly hesitantly. Barely had she set foot back on British soil from her short trip to Africa for a crisis meeting with Ma'Dika, she was summoned by Abaddon and hauled to his office by the Libabes XXX. Abaddon had made no attempt to contact Angelique and gave her personal space since her temporary betrothing to Santiago. Hence, no wonder she was concerned with the sudden apparition in her living room of the Abaddon's mystic beasts known as Libabes XXX. They had been expressly sent by the master to fetch her. Angelique quivered inside, it was synonymous of a bad omen that Abaddon had especially selected those creatures to escort her to him.

"Here she comes, my lovely Angelique. You are glowing. L'amour vous va si bien" hailed Abaddon with a hint of sarcasm as she entered the room. Angelique had her medium length ombré extension down. She sported a pair of skinny jeans, white t-shirt and platform trainers. The look was completed with a black leather biker jacket. She looked fresh, playful and carefree. Abaddon felt a pinch of jealousy that Santiago was now the one in her bed.

The chamber was a small cell like office Abaddon often used to hold meetings with subordinates he wanted to reprimand. Abaddon was in his human form with his black hair melting into the atmosphere. Dressed in black cassock, he stood behind his desk, with his hands on the table and ordered Angelique to take a seat opposite him. The Libabes XXX took their positions on either side of Abaddon. Angelique felt rather intimidated and extremely nervous.

"Hi Abaddon, is there any problem?" enquired Angelique in an attempt to sound as relaxed as possible.

"A problem? Whatever makes you ask this question?"

"No particular reason, just we have never had a meeting here before, that's all," Angelique replied nervously.

Abaddon was devouring Angelique with his eyes while caressing his bottom lip with his finger. "Tell me ma belle, how are things going with our dashing Santiago? He asked.

"Err...we are very happy," stuttered Angelique.

"Good! You know I care about your happiness," snapped Abaddon. That was such a big lie and Angelique knew it. Abaddon couldn't care less about anyone's happiness and he had no perception nor experience of what happiness actually was. In Angelique's mind, this conversation was getting more bizarre with every passing minute. Abaddon was taunting her.

"By the way, how's the Kasai assignment progressing?" Abaddon inquired, suddenly changing the topic.

Ah! She got it! This is what Abaddon was getting to. The purpose for the meeting became instantly clear to Angelique. She had to give careful thought to how she answered that question.

"Well, as you know this is a rather challenging project. However, I do expect positive results."

"Alright, what type of challenges are you facing? Anything I need to know?"

This was turning into a police interrogation scenario. It was obvious Abaddon knew something was wrong guessed Angelique. How though? She wondered. She pulled herself back together as this was not the time to try to figure that out, she needed to determine first her reply to Abaddon.

"Abaddon, missions like this sometimes suffer setbacks, but there is nothing I cannot handle. I am happy with the progress made."

"Hmm ok, smart answer. Bring in our guest!" he ordered and one of the libabes XXX opened the side door making way for none other than Greta Janssen. Before she could reconcile her presence in her head, Angelique noticed Greta held someone on a chain leash. To Angelique's choking horror that someone was none other than her father! He was on his knees with his head bowed down, he had a spiked iron collar fastened around his neck in the manner of slaves.

Angelique leapt from her chair and turned to Abaddon, "What is the meaning of this?" Greta had a smirk on her face. Revenge had never tasted so sweet, she was relishing every single minute of it.

"I am going to ask you one more time. How is the Kasai assignment progressing?" barked Abaddon, hitting the table with fists.

Angelique's entire body was shaking, a myriad of thoughts swirled around in her mind, and she began to fumble on her words, "We still have time to remedy the situation, I have a plan. Why does she have my father?"

"Because there is one point you conveniently failed to mention. One of my Libabe has gone missing!" Abaddon drew closer to Angelique and held her by the chin. "This, my dear, is a reminder of the consequences of trying to deceive me. Did you seriously think you could lose one of my libabes and I would not find out about it?"

Angelique attempted to plead with Abaddon and justify her actions, but he refused to heed her.

The scene of a begging and helpless Angelique provided Greta with immense satisfaction. Carla's lead turned out to be a gold mine. It did not take Greta a lot of work to uncover Angelique's big assignment to the Kasai region. She still had her sources in the circle of sages, many of whom she shared mutual friends with. Armed with the intel that Angelique had suffered a major setback in her Kasai assignment was enough to sow a seed of suspicion in Abaddon who was in the dark about Angelique's predicament. The rest was history. Abaddon took it from there and ended up discovering that a libabe had gone missing during one of Angelique's operations. Each time a libabe or an underworld creature was reported as vanished was when apprehended by the 'fishers'. Non-human underworld creatures captured by the 'fishers' were never seen again. Therefore, Abaddon took their disappearance personally, considering it an affront and insult to his person. Hence the very fact that Angelique had failed to mention the disappearance of an underworld creature was sufficient enough to arouse

Abaddon's rage against her. She had betrayed him by keeping silent on the matter.

At this point Angelique was on her knees at Abaddon's feet, "I don't know what happened to him, he vanished. But I will find him, I promise, please Abaddon this has nothing to do with my father."

"No, you are wrong my dear, you father is my collateral. You get me back my libabe if you can and Greta here will release you father who, as we speak, is now her personal slave," said Abaddon with a low chilling voice. With a glance at Greta who unlocked the collar from Richard's neck.

Before Angelique could figure out what was coming next, she heard Greta's sharp voice command Richard to strike Angelique on the cheek. Richard had no choice but to obey. He slapped his daughter.

This act was beyond painful for Angelique. It was not the physical rather the emotional abuse and humiliation she and Richard were subjected to. Tears were streaming down on both of their faces. This was Greta's moment of triumph and she was savouring every second of it. She ordered Richard to strike Angelique one more time. Richard was her slave now, she could do with him whatever she desired. Her assertiveness and astuteness in acting on Carla's information had paid off. She knew exactly how Abaddon would grant her any wish as a reward for the information she provided. Richard was the recompense she requested. Such a sweet recompense... A double whammy coming in the form of a sex slave she had converted Richard into and the torture Angelique would endure knowing that her dearest father was a puppet in the hands of her greatest enemy. For a split second her thoughts wandered on all the dirty things she had in store for Richard.

"Another faux pas and it shall be worse," warned Abaddon before dismissing Angelique.

Being on the receiving hand of the underworld's cruelty was a new experience for Angelique. She did not like it one bit. She was hurt and infuriated at the same time. At the very first opportunity, Angelique vowed within herself she will make Greta pay handsomely for this humiliating act. But, first things first and at the top of the list was Rachel Parker who was fast turning into her nemesis. She had to get her out of the way, no matter what the costs.

Chapter 32
Angelique Strikes

"Mi amor despertate, wake up mi amor." Santiago was gently shaking Angelique. She got up gasping, sat up on the bed with a hand on her heart, trembling.

Santiago amorously placed his arms around her shoulders, "amor, you were speaking in your sleep, you were agonizing," he said, kissing her on the temple and caressing her hair.

"I had the most peculiar dream, Santi. I was a fish in the ocean and got caught with many other fish in a net. The fishing net was pulled through the water on a boat. There was a man, whose face I could not see, because the sun was on his face. He was the one who was examining all the fish for defects or signs of ill health and deciding whether to destroy or keep them. When it was my turn, I heard a voice coming from the bottom of the ocean saying that one is Angelique Sakola she deserves death. When I heard what that voice said, I started flapping trying to beg for mercy, but the words weren't coming out of my mouth, and you woke me up," recounted Angelique.

Santiago paused a few seconds and said, "I am no expert on the subject but I have read that dreams are often a reflection of our state of mind and I know you have been quite pre-occupied recently with your assignment, so it could be the stress getting to you."

"You might be right babe, it's doing my head in," agreed Angelique. She rested her head on his shoulder and wrapped her arms around his waist.

Santiago reciprocated her hug. "I don't like seeing you like this. Let me know what I can do to help you?"

"This is something I have to do on my own, besides you have your own assignment to complete."

"I completed mine a couple of days ago, let me help you," insisted Santiago.

Angelique was adamant. "This is between Rachel and I. Don't worry I'll get the better of her."

Santiago gave in. "Fine, que terca eres, you are so stubborn. But let me at least give you some Colombian love boost." He rolled her over onto the bed laughing then kissed her neck before making his way onto her lips for a passionate embrace which culminated in crazy mind-blowing lovemaking.

Santiago's Colombian love boost worked. Angelique felt energised and ready for the next round with Rachel. This tug of war had reached a critical stage, there was no room for error. She had to plan her attack meticulously. To boost her chances of success, she carried out further research on Rachel before launching her attack. Interestingly, on paper there was nothing about Rachel that would pose a threat to Angelique. She led a normal life, she had no involvement with the underworld, nor magic. She attended the fishers' group gatherings on a regular basis. These gatherings which revolved around their dead and alive ruler had nothing of notable significance Angelique thought. This, however, left

Angelique more perplexed because she could not comprehend where their powers came from. She could not logically join the dots about Rachel and was intrigued about the hedge of fire that surrounded her. This new form of protection was alien to Angelique and how on earth such an ordinary woman with nebulous powers managed to obstruct her entire operation left Angelique stumped.

Notwithstanding, Angelique was determined to finish with Rachel once and for all and was ready to utilise the highest level of magic to destroy her enemy. In that respect she entered into the deepest meditation and fasting mode by retreating in the third layer of the Amazon bottom set river bed for three days. That form of extreme isolation enabled her to harness all her energy and power with the sole objective of bringing about the death of Rachel Parker.

Once fully loaded with all mystical powers to the maximum, Angelique's strategy was to attack Rachel in the middle of night while she was asleep, at around three a.m. which is known as witch hour. This was the time where the forces of darkness operated at a higher level of intensity. For additional reinforcement, she even requested from Abaddon the assistance of thirteen Libabes XXX to support her mission, which Abaddon agreed to. Though he did not openly admit to Angelique, Abaddon was cognisant of the mammoth challenge facing Angelique.

At exactly three a.m. Angelique astral projected with her company heading for Rachel's house in Chicago, USA. The plan was to directly land by the bedside of the target and deliver her fatal blow.

On this occasion, however, although she and the Libabes XXX landed inside Rachel's bedroom, they felt constrained to stand by the door. Some force she could not see prevented them from moving closer to the bed. Angelique figured it was the hedge Ma'Dika warned her about.

From where Angelique and the Libabe XXX stood, it was impossible to see Rachel. There were thirty-two shining tall men dressed in white standing by Rachel's bed. They stood shoulder to shoulder, arms linked, thus creating an unbreakable circle around Rachel's bed. The countenance of their apparel was dazzling to the extent that Rachel and the Libabes XXX had to cover their eyes and were unable to see past them. Angelique also noticed that they had wings and their feet never touched the ground. She could not help but marvel at the sight of these creatures she was seeing for the first time in her life. It also briefly crossed her mind, as stood there dressed in black rags, how filthy and repulsive she and the Libabes XXX looked in comparison. These men appeared extremely strong and powerful, yet they exuded peace and serenity, contrary to all the creatures in the underworld who embodied dread and doom. The features of their faces were handsome but expressionless. Their raised swords were used to fend off attacks from Angelique and her army of Libabes XXX who were sent off, flying, falling on their back powerless whenever they tried to advance. After around five unsuccessful attempts, Angelique began to realise she was dealing with a much stronger opponent. As she pondered on her next move, another creature who also looked like a man, descended from above into the bedroom. He was very tall, four-winged and his strength and authority filled the room. His face had the appearance of the sun. He was clothed in white and gold shining armour and held a golden sword. As he descended, his feet, which were like fiery pillars, stopped a few centimetres from the ground as he gently hovered over the surface. He was magnificent. Never had Angelique seen a more perfect creature, she guessed he was the commander of the group.

He looked straight at Angelique, his eyes were like flames of fire and as he opened his mouth to speak, his voice resembled the sound of an earthquake.

"Who are you looking for, Angelique Sakola?" he asked.

How come he knew her name, Angelique wondered. She was intimidated, but nevertheless Angelique mustered some courage, "We are here for Rachel, and we won't leave until we see her!"

"It is not permitted for you to see Rachel, please leave," he commanded with authority.

At this point Angelique knew she was fighting a losing battle. However, the image of her father in bondage along with the punishment that awaited if she failed forced her to keep insisting.

"I know Rachel is here," insisted Angelique. "If you do not move out of our way, we'll be forced to harm you," she threatened. She thought she sounded ridiculous. These men were clearly stronger than they were.

"You know you have no power over us. Go home Angelique," he said firmly with determination in his eyes. Refusing to accept defeat, Angelique decided to give it another try and turned to the Libabes XXX, "Move this dude out of my way!" she commanded. At her command, the Libabes XXX dared not attack, they were frozen and seemed petrified since the apparition of the four-winged man. They looked like scared goons.

"Did you hear me?" shouted Angelique in desperation. There was no reaction from the Libabes XXX.

In retaliation the commander gave the order to apprehend the Libabes XXX, who were seized and dragged into the unknown by thirteen of the shining men.

"Now do you understand there is nothing you can do against us?" the commander asked Angelique, who was left alone in the room.

"I am not leaving until I see Rachel, I know she is here." The thought of returning defeated was not an option for Angelique. She would rather die than fail in her mission for a second time.

"What do you want with Rachel?" asked the commander.

"It's got nothing to do with you! Get out of my way!" she yelled.

Before Angelique could make another move, the commander lifted his index finger and, as he pointed toward her, he released a force which elevated Angelique in the air and thrust her against the wall.

"Go home Angelique and consider your ways," he said.

The only ways she had to consider was how to get rid of Rachel Parker, Angelique thought. "I will reward you handsomely if you join me," offered Angelique as she struggled to get back on her feet.

"My master is greater than yours, isn't it obvious to you?"

Actually she hated to admit it, but he might be right. Hence before bowing out, she decided to seek the identity of this great master who so humiliated her.

"What is the name of your master?" she asked the commander.

"He is the one who was dead and now is alive, his name is The Bright Morning Star. He sent us to camp around Rachel and protect her from your evil intentions because she is beloved. The Bright Morning Star is all-knowing, all-powerful and ever-present," he replied.

Who was that Star? And how come Angelique had never heard of him and these shining creatures who somehow seemed to know her. They radiated with a light that Angelique had never seen before in her life. For the first time since being crowned one of the most powerful witches in the universe, Angelique faced greater powers than the magic of the underworld.

Her world had just been turned upside down. Forced to concede, Angelique glanced one last time at the four-winged commander and flew out through Rachel's bedroom window. Rachel had won. Angelique not only had lost this battle, but the capture of the Libabes XXX would aggravate her misery and cost her dearly. She was filled with that sentiment of dread and anxiety that a major storm was heading her way and there was nothing she could do to avoid it.

ISABELLE KAMALANDWA BRYAN

Chapter 33
The Punishment

When Angelique informed Abaddon that she had failed again, he did not send Libabe XXX to fetch her, but he personally chose to pay Angelique a visit at her apartment in London at exactly midnight. Having resigned to her fate, Angelique waited for him as a prisoner on death row awaits the executioner's fatal blow sitting still on her sofa. Abaddon had brought along his cohort of sages and together they subjected Angelique to the vilest kind of chastisement that can be inflicted on a woman. At their hand she suffered the most vicious kind of sexual abuse which lasted until the early hours of the morning.

Santiago and Arjun were both compelled by Abaddon to participate against their will in the act which was emotionally devastating for Angelique. Abaddon had succeeded in debasing her friendship with Arjun – she would never look at Jashwanti in the same way – and made a dent in her love story with Santiago. The trio knew they would have to rise above this incident and move on. But exactly how to do so was the question none of them had the answer to.

The road to recovery was an arduous one in the aftermath of the abuse for Angelique. Santiago showed tender loving care for Angelique and was extremely attentive to her needs. He opted to remain with her on that fatal night after Abaddon and the sages departed in the early hours of the morning; helping her bathe and tucked her in bed. Santiago's heart went out to Angelique and her traumatic experience. As a sage the act did not shock him because brutality in any shape or form was their way of life. The complexity Santiago was facing however was about how to reconcile in his mind his girlfriend's rape which although he hated to acknowledge had left him emotionally disturbed. To avoid further upsetting Angelique, he kept his feelings to himself.

Although he made an effort to repress his feelings, Santiago felt humiliated and debased by Abaddon in a way he never experienced before. It was a show of power and Abaddon's way to remind him that he was master of both Angelique and him and they were mere puppets in his hands. This unfamiliar, yet familiar, face of underworld reality was a bitter pill for Santiago to swallow.

Angelique on the other hand, decided she would do her best to avoid Arjun and Jashwanti. She could not bring herself to face her best friend. Debauchery and promiscuity were the trademarks of the underworld, so while it would not be a big deal for Angelique to have sex with Arjun, the rules were different because he was her best friend's husband and hence off limits. Abuse or not, her friendship with Jahwanti would be ruined forever if she was to find out.

In one night, as with a magic wand, Abaddon had wreaked havoc on her two most precious relationships. Angelique abhorred what had happened but she had to face the facts that she was part of a world where such occurrences were common practice. Cruelty was its foundation. Cruelty was normal. She had to pick herself up and move on. At least she still had Santiago and did not have to put up with Abaddon's night visits.

Angelique kept her fingers crossed Santiago would be able to brush this incident under the carpet and in time both of their wounds would heal.

ISABELLE KAMALANDWA BRYAN

Chapter 34
Who Is the Bright Morning Star?

In the underworld you never abandon a mission, you keep going until you either win or die. Although Angelique had lost the battle against Rachel, the war was by no means over. Rachel was her nemesis and Angelique would not rest until she brought her down. Angelique had a powerful incentive that kept her motivated: her father's freedom. Abaddon had clearly laid the rules, conditioning Richard's release from Greta's grip upon the delivery of the head of Rachel Parker. She was given eighteen months, after which time if she did not succeed, the Kasai operation would be assigned to another sage and she would be terminated in the physical world and banished to the underworld metropolis as a slave. In the meantime and luckily for Angelique, Santiago had managed to secure a smaller ore of diamonds in Venezuela, which enabled Abaddon to push forward with the manufacturing of his chip. The deposit in Venezuela was due to run out in exactly eighteen months.

The news about Angelique's crisis spread like wildfire in the underworld. All eyes were on her, especially those of the young witches who awaited nothing but her downfall. Angelique vowed to rise above her predicament. Her first move was to inflict the same level of chastisement to her team. No one fails a mission and remains unpunished. Angelique ordered a group of wicked warlocks to sexually abuse Jen. Then, she orchestrated an assault on General Mbuyi by the Libabes. The general was so severely battered to the point of death that he needed intensive care for a couple of months.

Next, Angelique proceeded to devote more time gathering intel about the fishers, the source of their power and their master 'The Bright Morning Star'. She enlisted the support of Ma'Dika in that endeavour. Together they visited the prestigious underworld library in search for some clues and data from magic books written by ancient wizards on that matter. It was during their perusing of ancient magic literature that they came across scrolls by a diviner named Balaam, the son of Beor, the destroyer of the people. In his inscription 'The Heresy of Peor' Balaam described an ancient people against whom there was no sorcery nor any divination. Like the fishers these people referred to as 'The Elect' were surrounded with an unbreakable hedge. This protection extended to family members also. Three times the diviner attempted to curse 'The Elect' without success. Their protection was impenetrable to the extent that curses pronounced would bounce back to the originator. Angelique was about to despair while reading when the diviner advised the reader that he had found a way to curse 'The Elect'. The diviner discovered in the ancient days that unlike any other mortals, 'The Elect' could only be cursed if there was a cause. Without a cause the curse against the 'The Elect' would not function. A cause was described as an act by which 'The Elect' entered into agreement either intentionally or unintentionally with the underworld practises. This could be achieved by luring the Elect to partake in magic and commit sexual perversion. These acts would prompt the downfall of the Elect and cause the hedge to break.

Angelique was fascinated by the inscription. "What does the diviner mean by sexual perversion?" Angelique asked Ma'Dika.

"The power of the Elect dwelt in their purity and sexual activity had to be confined within the bounds of marriage. So, if they were to engage in a sex act outside of marriage that would count as sexual perversion," explained Ma'Dika.

At last, Angelique got the sensation that there was a light at the end of this tunnel. Balaam, the son of Beor, had provided her with some ammunition for a second round against Rachel Parker. Interestingly, however, there was no information about The Bright Morning Star to be found anywhere across the extensive portfolio of manuscripts stored in the prestigious library.

Although armed with a vital piece of information, Angelique was in no hurry to launch a second attack. A detailed plan of action had to be elaborated on, the best approach decided. She intended to allocate sufficient time to carefully strategise. She was conscious that Rachel would not easily be enticed to commit those acts. In that respect, Ma'Dika advised her that the most effective method would be to weaken Rachel by causing chaos around her. Ma'Dika elucidated, "It has been known that very often pain and suffering weakens the mind, compromises rationality and drives people to uncharacteristic behaviour." Therefore, the best way to weaken Rachel was by also targeting her beloved children and using them as a way of entry to get to Rachel.

Angelique reconvened with Jen to share her vision of adopting a different tactic in their battle against Rachel. She was wary not to disclose the source of her new finding and ensured that she would drip feed her information as they progress in their mission. In the interim, she tasked Jen with carrying out some research on Rachel Parker's immediate family including her children.

Finally, Angelique felt she personally needed to get to know Rachel a little bit better. And the best way to do it was to spy on her. She decided to put her shape shifting skills to use by transforming into a black cat to enable her to visit Rachel's residence once a week without suspicion. A cherry blossom tree located in Rachel's five-hundred square foot front yard garden in the suburbs of west side Chicago became her perfect observing spot. The tree was tall enough to give Angelique a good view on the rooms inside the two-storey property. Hence, she could perch on top of the tree and record Rachel's activities once a week. Every now and then she would venture closer to the property. That approach turned out to be quite risky because Rachel had a dog that would chase her away every time. Angelique hated that dog.

Her snooping escapades enabled Angelique to get better acquainted with her opponent. It was during those stake outs, that she discovered that Rachel had very few friends. The only frequent visitor she had was Lucy O'Connor, her personal assistant, who also seemed to be her only close friend. The people who mattered the most to her were her two children and she devoted much of her time to looking after them. She enjoyed walking her dog in the nearby park. She did not date and came across as a private person.

It was her spirituality which was more intriguing to Angelique. For a woman with her powers Angelique expected to witness deep spiritual activities such as astral projections, or conjuration of spirits and there was none of that with Rachel. Three times a week she went to the gym and once a week she held a meeting in her house with some boring looking people during which there was a lot of reading based on one book, called the 'sacred writings'. At the weekend she attended a congregation meeting with other fellow fishers in downtown Chicago. In the underworld, it was strictly forbidden to consult the 'sacred writings', hence no copies could be found in that part of the universe. All wizards and witches were warned the 'sacred writing' was a corrupt book and championed the doctrine of the fishers which was in direct contradiction with the underworld. Anyone found reading that book faced severe ramifications in the underworld.

The more Angelique was finding out about Rachel's mundane life, the more she was intrigued by her.

Chapter 35
Goodbye Love

Christmas was around the corner and it had been about six months since Angelique's romance with Santiago began. Angelique was keen to continue the relationship and hoped Santiago felt the same way. She felt slightly worried that he had not brought up the topic with the end date for their romance looming so close. In an effort to get Santiago to make some form of commitment, Angelique invited herself to his hacienda in Argentina over the festive season. Lately, cartel related rivalries in South America, had kept Santiago from travelling to Europe to see Angelique. She had ditched her mother's invitation for a family Christmas in favour of some time with Santiago and felt not an inkling of remorse because she did not like Christmas anyway. In her opinion it was an elaborated PR machine coaxing unsuspecting consumers to shop until they drop.

La Piedad was a one hundred and fifty year old hacienda situated in La Rioja province in West Argentina that belonged to Santiago. He used the hacienda as a place of retreat and tranquility. It was perfectly positioned at the foot of a hill, extending over forty hectares of land with breathtaking views of the vineyard and surrounding hills. On Christmas morning Angelique went for a run. The weather was particularly pleasant and warm. December is the summer season in Argentina. Santiago was still in bed when Angelique returned from her morning jog. He looked incredibly sexy lying on the bed asleep, breathing gently. After a quick quiet shower, she slid her wet freshly showered body under the covers pressing it seductively against Santiago's. The feeling of Angelique's body against his woke Santiago up.

"Good morning you," whispered a half-asleep Santiago pulling Angelique even closer.

"Hola," she replied, planting a kiss on his lips. That was an invitation he could not refuse.

He made love to her over and over again on that Christmas morning. They shared a shower afterwards where there was more lovemaking. Finally, when they emerged from the bedroom at about noon, they went on the hacienda veranda for a late breakfast consisting of fruits, coffee and pastries. The aroma of freshly-brewed coffee freely circulated in the hacienda and was enhanced delicately by the mild regional breeze. Curled up against Santiago's chest on a large swing chair and hearing his heartbeat was pure bliss for Angelique. Santiago was all she wanted for Christmas.

"I could not think of a better way to say goodbye darling," said Santiago as he pressed his lips on her forehead. The writing was on the wall and Santiago was conscious he had to face this moment, sooner or later. He owed it to Angelique to let her know in person that he would not pursue their relationship.

Angelique looked up at him with doves' eyes, "What do you mean, are you travelling?"

"No amor, remember our six months are up in a couple of days."

He was not telling her anything new, her intention was to

discuss with him how they'd carry on and not say goodbye.

"Yes, I know. It has gone so fast and I've loved every single moment we spent together. I don't want it to end. Will you seek an extension?" queried Angelique innocently.

Santiago hesitated, he did not like the thought of hurting her but he had to stick to his guns and end the relationship. However much he tried he could not see a way forward. What they had was not sustainable.

"It was good while it lasted. I'll have fond memories of us," he replied, placing his hand on her cheek, looking straight into her eyes.

Santiago was not lying, what he had experienced with Angelique was unforgettable and he gladly would have wanted it to continue, but he feared an extension request would turn him into Abaddon's rival for Angelique's affections. That was dangerous grounds.

"Santi baby, it does not have to end. If it is about the dowry, I'll help you get the souls," pleaded Angelique. She did not want to return to Abaddon.

Santiago stood up, ran his hand in his hair nervously before asserting, "Angelique, it's not just the next six months, but it's the months after and the ones after that. Besides, Abaddon may decide to increase the dowry for all we know. The entire situation is untenable. So it's better to finish before we get too entangled." He really was trying hard to make Angelique understand. It was difficult enough for Santiago to let go of her.

On her side, Angelique recollected there was something different about Santiago's lovemaking in the morning. There was such intensity and emotions involved and the number of times they made love that morning was very unusual. It dawned on her that he was actually saying goodbye.

Angelique snapped and pounced on Santiago screaming and hitting him in the chest. "You jerk, you only wanted sex with me and you made sure you had some before dumping me!"

Santiago restrained her by holding her wrists, "Angelique please believe me, I am not dumping you, you belong to someone else and you will never be mine!" He felt his eyes tingle, his heart was hurting.

Santiago was right, she belonged to Abaddon, the best he could ever do is borrow her but she will never be his. Angelique paused and calmed herself down and could hardly believe herself the words that were to come out of her mouth; "Let's run away!"

Santiago was shocked. "Have you lost your mind, we are not in a romance novel."

"If you feel strongly enough for me, we could find a way to..."

Santiago had strong feelings for her, but deep down he knew this would never work as long as Abaddon, the ruler of the underworld, was her husband and an extremely jealous one for that matter. So he interrupted Angelique before she could complete her sentence and scolded her, "Enough Angelique, this is our world, this is what we do and who we are! There is no way out. It's for life. Get a grip on yourself!"

Angelique sat back down on the swing chair. "Santiago, would you have considered my proposal crazy if I had not been raped?"

"That incident has got nothing to do with this. Didn't my actions prove it to you? The reality is that you belong to Abaddon and that's it," he replied, kneeling down and touching both her hands. Truly enough, Angelique's rape was a hard pill to swallow but that did not change how felt about her.

The morning that started so beautifully in 'La Rioja' ended as a disaster. Fate had given Angelique one more reason to hate Christmas. With no valid reason to hang around in the hacienda, although Santiago insisted she could stay as long as she wished, Angelique caught the first flight back to London on Boxing Day. Her heart was shattered into pieces.

She had lost the man who made her happy and now had to go back in the arms of Abaddon. Angelique blamed Rachel Parker. That woman was the cause of all her misery. The sooner she would get rid of her the better she thought.

Chapter 36
Brownie's Triumph

A good workout was just what Rachel needed. Now a woman in her early forties, Rachel was keen to keep fit and stay healthy. Kevin, her new personal trainer, was a great motivator and a genius. Thanks to his tailor-made fitness plan she had managed to tone up her entire body enhancing her enviable silhouette and at the same time increase her energy levels in merely three months. Moreover, he was such an adorable person. He constantly showered Rachel with compliments which made her feel really good about herself. At first Rachel thought it was his way to boost his clients' self-confidence, but later found out he had a different rapport with his other clients.

On his part, Kevin went out of his way to give Rachel multiple subtle hints that he was interested. However, uncertain about how she would react to his advances and keen to protect their professional relationship he stopped short of asking her out. He was hopeful Rachel would pick up his signals and take the initiative, to which he would reciprocate immediately.

Rachel most definitely picked up Kevin cheeky suggestive innuendos. She was flattered that a man a decade younger was showing a romantic interest in her. Although Rachel was not insensitive to Kevin's charms – for he was a very attractive man – she could not turn a blind eye on the reality of her forty-two years of age and his thirty-one. The age gap made her slightly uncomfortable. She was tempted but doubted they had much in common outside their workout sessions and their budding mutual physical attraction. Deep down she felt a little out of his league and intimidated by his gorgeousness. Rachel had lost count of the number of pretty young girls who were after him.

The death was hugely devastating for Rachel. For a long time she was unable to connect emotionally with the opposite sex. She instead focused all her energy on her children and her work.

As the years passed, her children grew up. David, her eldest, recently moved out of the family home into his own apartment in downtown Chicago, while Jessica was getting ready to go to college. Her children's newly-gained independence brought to the surface her loneliness and the desire she had long ignored to be with somebody. A bit of harmless flirting with her personal trainer made her feel beautiful and rejuvenated. However, she had no plan to take it further and a harmless flirt is what it shall remain.

Rachel was deep in her thoughts when she entered her house through the kitchen door. The last thing she expected was to see Lucy waiting for her sitting comfortably at the kitchen table sipping a glass of milk. Rachel was startled, she initially took her for a burglar.

"Oh my God Lucy, you gave me such a scare!! How did you get in?"

Lucy dangled a set of keys above her head, "You gave copies, remember?"

"Yes I forgot. I did not know you were coming."

"Sorry about that. But I wanted to personally deliver to you the research piece on WAXXA." Lucy pulled out the A4 Report Project Document Files Folder and handed it over to Rachel whose face lit up.

"Splendid! Finally! Thanks for bringing it over. This might provide some clarity on why WAXXA are so hell-bent on acquiring Ndeko mines."

Lucy observed Rachel getting excited like a little girl who had just received a box of candies.

"You are welcome, although I would put the brakes on the enthusiasm if I were you, there is not much info out there about WAXXA. It's almost like they are some type of cult or secret society."

Rachel quickly flicked through the dossier. "I know and I think there is something that does not square up with that bank. I have never felt this level of spiritual attack. First it was the militia's attack and then a couple of months ago, the most evil presence entered my room. I could not see what it was but all I could sense was light around me, protecting me. Hopefully this report might have some type of clue."

"I hope you find some answers and remember we are on the winning side, always," said Lucy squeezing Rachel's hand tightly.

"Yes we are," affirmed Rachel with a soft smile.

"By the way changing topics, you are looking great. Have you just come from the gym, how was it?"

"It was hard work but worth it. Kevin is a sweetheart."

"This is about the third time I have heard about this new fitness instructor of yours. If I did not know you better I'd say you have a bit of a crush."

"Actually, I think he is hitting on me," confessed a blushing Rachel.

"Maybe it's about time you gave love a chance," advised Lucy whose attention was caught by something else. She leaned forward to look through the blinds of the kitchen window, "By the way your dog hasn't stopped barking."

Rachel also looked out of the window into the garden, "You're right, I hear him too. Don't know why Brownie is acting up. About love, not sure, he is eleven years younger than me."

"I know it's a cliché, but they say age is nothing but a number. If you don't try you won't know. You have been alone for as long as I have known you Rachel," Lucy placed a hand on Rachel's shoulder in a bid to provide some friendly comfort to her friend and boss.

"Aside from the age gap, we probably have incompatible goals and values. And I have children, he doesn't," counter-argued Rachel attempting to make her case.

"I won't insist, I just want to see you happy," said Lucy as she gave Rachel a big hug.

"I know and I appreciate it," replied Rachel hugging Lucy back.

"I have to go now. It's getting late," said Lucy and she gently pulled away.

"Sure, I will walk you out and check what has got Brownie

in such a state."

After closing the gate behind Lucy, Rachel made her way toward the front garden. As she got closer, she could not shake an eerie sensation that something bizarre was going on.

Life was a funny thing. She was one of the most influential businesswomen on the planet, people envied her and many wanted to be her. Those people should see her now, perched on a tree with a stupid dog that would not stop barking. Dogs had an ability to smell witches and this bichon frisée was doing an amazing job at it. He had been sniffing and barking around the tree where Angelique was for the past 10 minutes. Stupid dog! Angelique had multiplied her surveillance activities since her split with Santiago. Someone would have thought a woman of her stature would have more exciting things to do. Well, her life was not that exciting, it just looked the part. She was just faking it in the hope she would make it.

She was about to give that stupid dog a little scare black magic style when she heard Rachel's voice shout, "Brownie! Stop all that noise!"

Brownie even barked more vigorously wagging its tail frantically as if he was calling his mistress to come over and see what he had discovered. Rachel did exactly that and came to the bottom of the tree and started patting Brownie to calm him down. Then she looked up and saw what got Brownie so excited, it was a black cat. The spirit of the Bright Morning Star whispered to her that the cat was in fact Angelique. Rachel looked intensely at that cat and said, "You have been coming here and disturbing my dog. So come down from that tree Angelique!"

Wait a minute! Did she just call her by her name Angelique? Now Angelique was spooked and she is the one who usually does the spooking.

Rachel kept talking, "Angelique I know it's you, come down!"

Angelique was not about to blow her cover and there was no way she was coming down.

"Angelique Sakola, in the name of The Bright Morning Star, come down now!" ordered Rachel.

Angelique felt every fibre in her body compelled to obey. She dropped down from the tree like a lump of dough. Her shape shifting dissipated and she laid butt naked on Rachel's damp lawn in her human form. Brownie barked in triumph, this is what he was trying to tell his mistress all along. Angelique was attempting with little success to cover her nudity. This was embarrassing. Unexpectedly, Rachel helped her get up. "Come inside, I'll give you something to wear," offered Rachel.

Reluctantly Angelique followed Rachel inside the house. Brownie was proudly trotting along by Rachel's side.

There was Angelique in her arch enemy's kitchen naked. That was now beyond embarrassing, it was plain awkward.

"A glass of orange juice?" offered Rachel.

Now she was offering her a drink. She would have preferred something stronger, but a juice would do. She felt as weak as a baby, all her powers were drained out of her and she was parched.

Rachel served Angelique a large glass of orange juice

with ice and grabbed a long tee-shirt from the dryer which she handed to Angelique. She invited Angelique to sit opposite her across her kitchen table. Brownie parked by his mistress's chair kept a watchful eye on Angelique.

Rachel was very calm. Angelique would have expected she'd throw a tantrum but that was not the case. She looked so sure of herself, she was in command of the situation.

"Interesting meeting under such circumstances Angelique. The last time I saw you, you looked more elegant than this," said Rachel.

"How did you know the cat was me?" asked Angelique.

"There is nothing hidden in my world," replied Rachel.

"What world is this?"

"One better than yours."

"There are no greater powers than those of the underworld."

"So how come you are the one naked in my kitchen?"

Angelique had no reply to that question, but she was not about to give Rachel the satisfaction to witness her perplexity.

"Sooner or later I will get you Rachel!" she threatened defiantly.

"Don't you dare threaten me in my own kitchen! No weapon formed against me shall ever prosper," retorted Rachel calmly.

Those words shot through Angelique in her inner core and froze her. She felt powerless against this woman. Yes! She was confused.

"My master will deal with you," warned Angelique.

"No weapon formed against me shall prosper," repeated Rachel. "Besides my Master is greater than your master."

She heard that before. Angelique smirked, "Who? That Bright Morning Star who was dead and alive?"

"Yes, The Bright Morning Star. You should consider switching camps. He is a lot nicer than your wicked master."

What did this woman know about her life anyway and Abaddon? How dare Rachel talk to her in that manner? Before Angelique could reply, Rachel continued, "By the way, I know all this shenanigan is about Ndeko mines. Why do you want our business so badly that you would come after me like this?"

Angelique riposted defiantly, "I want it because no one turns me down. I always get what I want!"

Rachel stood up from her chair, placed both hands on the table. Her expression was not as friendly anymore, she rebuked her severely, "Listen to me carefully Angelique Sakola, you will never get your hands on Ndeko and you'd better rethink your evil plans concerning my person. I suggest you move on and don't ever come back to my house again, because next time there will be fire waiting for you. Now be on your way!" Rachel pointed in the direction of the door.

It was the most humbling experience of Angelique's life. It

was easy enough for Rachel to tell her to move on, thought Angelique. She had no idea what was at stake, firstly the release of Angelique's father. Secondly, Angelique's own life was at stake. The quarrel had turned into a personal power struggle between the two women. This war was far from over. As far as Angelique was concerned it had just begun. For now, Angelique would patiently suffer the shame. She exited Rachel's house head down under Brownie's jubilant barks. She gathered up just enough strength to project back to England and flew off. But in the words of the terminator; "She will be back!"

The End of Part I

ISABELLE KAMALANDWA BRYAN

About the Author

Isabelle Kamalandwa Bryan is originally from the Democratic Republic of Congo. She is passionate about Human Rights and currently develops income strategies for a global anti-trafficking organisation. She also serves as a board member for an NGO which supports street children in Congo. Isabelle loves to travel and write poetry.

ISABELLE KAMALANDWA BRYAN

About PublishU

PublishU is transforming the world of publishing.

PublishU has developed a new and unique approach to publishing books, offering a three-step guided journey to becoming a globally published author!

We enable hundreds of people a year to write their book within 100-days, publish their book in 100-days and launch their book over 100-days to impact tens of thousands of people worldwide.

The journey is transformative, one author said,

"I never thought I would be able to write a book, let alone in 100 days… now I'm asking myself what else have I told myself that can't be done that actually can?'"

To find out more visit
www.PublishU.com

ISABELLE KAMALANDWA BRYAN